His Heart's Promise

A LETTING LOVE IN STORY
BOOK THREE

DAWN BACA

Dedication

To my darling husband Jeremy, without you there is only darkness. You shine a light on me with your love. I will always choose you. I am grateful every day for all that we have created in this life together.

And to Bob Decker and Danny Decker.
There are no others in this world that have known me longer or understood me better than the two of you. From the dark days of my childhood, to the years of growing and stumbling to find my way, you have always been there.
Your loving guidance means everything to me.
You are family.

Difficult roads often lead to beautiful destinations.

—— Anonymous

Contents

Dark Thoughts

Sophie

The stifling fog rolled in. It blanketed everything, leaving no visible light—like walking through a tunnel, no beginning, no end. Soundless, solemn, devoid of emotion. Not a single sensory impression.

A cocoon of mist surrounded Sophie, swallowing her in suffocating silence. The sense of dread permeated her every cell, rendering her unable to move. A sharp chill clawed its way into her bones, slicing clear through to her heart, leaving an agony so overwhelming it stole her ability to utter a sound.

An intense sensation of falling consumed her. Her stomach pitched, and she lurched. She reached out for him, her hand trembling, desperate for her lover, but her fingers landed on cold, lonely sheets. Her heart froze as the reality sank in.

He was gone.

Lost to her forever.

Despair flooded her. Peace shattered, the shards rained down around her as she screamed his name.

"Shh. Sweetheart, it's okay. I'm right here," Claude said.

Whipping her head toward his voice, she blinked, bringing the pitch-black room into dim focus. "Oh, Claude!" she cried.

He reached out and wrapped his arms tight around her as tears dripped down her cheeks and onto his bare chest.

Sweat trickled down her back, soaking into her silk nightgown and adding discomfort to the lingering fear. The inky darkness of the room reminded her too much of the smothering fog, setting her nerves even more on edge. Her head throbbed as she tried to wrap her mind around the dream.

The nightmare had come again. It swooped in, seizing her heaving lungs, and lodged her breath in her throat while her heartbeat pounded heavily in her ears. Gulping in air, she focused on breathing, trying to calm her queasy stomach.

She never knew where it came from. Some immeasurable, unconscious threat to her happiness brewed within. She couldn't put her finger on it, but deep down to her core, she knew without a doubt something was just not right.

Sophie clung to Claude as hot tears rolled down her cheek, soaking the hair next to her ear. Being held in his arms soothed her rattled soul. She so desperately wanted to chalk these horrid dreams up to pre-wedding jitters. She wasn't a particularly superstitious person, but there was just something about them which made it hard to do.

He caressed the back of her head, pulling away the hair matted to the side of her face. The gentle strokes lulled her into relaxing, and she sank further into him.

"Talk to me, *mon amour*. What has you so scared?" His hands caressed her arms, moving up and down, rubbing away the gooseflesh pebbling her skin.

Sophie gulped back the tears. "There are these dreams where I reach for you, and you're not there."

"But that is not unreasonable, we don't spend every night together." His tone was dismissive as he patted her back.

"*Non…*" She paused, taking a deep breath. It

filled her sore lungs with needle-like pricks. "It's hard to explain, but I sense it's more than just that."

"Oh, Soph, you worry too much. It's the wedding. You have to take a break from it. All this stress is not healthy."

His unenthusiastic response stopped Sophie short. The words died on her lips. There was no point protesting. If she couldn't make sense of the doom brewing within, how could she make him understand?

CHAPTER 1

Finding the One

Sophie

S ophie Compte sat beside her best friend, Addison Petrova, on the butter-soft leather sofa in the showroom of the most exclusive wedding dress boutique in Paris. The glare off the enormous rock on her left hand had her both flinching and biting back a grin. Claude had good taste. Not too flashy but enough weight to make her aware of the thing. Just what she liked. The five-carat, cushion-set, champagne-colored diamond sparkled under the fluorescent bulbs. Her engagement had been a long time coming, and now, with the ring securely on her finger, the race to plan her dream wedding began.

Unfortunately, she'd had anything but a smooth

start. She knew three things for sure. Claude was the man she was meant to marry. The wedding and reception would be held on her family's estate because it was dear to both her and her fiancé's hearts. And, over the last few months, she had become convinced she was never going to find the right dress to walk down the aisle in. Not that she hadn't tried.

Twisting the ring around her finger, lost in thought, she hadn't caught most of her friend's question.

"…and so of course Sergei shaved his head…" Addison said.

"Huh? What?"

Addison nudged her arm. "Where'd you go? You haven't heard a word I've said for the past five minutes."

"Hmm. I'm sorry. What did you say?" Sophie put her hands in her lap.

"What kind of dress do you have in mind?" Addison asked.

"I don't know." Sophie blew long bangs out of her eyes.

"What do you mean you don't know? How could you not know?"

"I know what I don't want, but I really am not

sure what I *do* want. I've tried on so many dresses already."

"How many is that?" Addison asked.

"Seventy-five? Eighty? Honestly, I've lost count."

Addison's mouth popped open. "Holy crap, Sophie! Who tries on that many dresses? Didn't you even look through wedding magazines first?"

"*Oui.* Since I was ten. But that doesn't help now. I've grown up," Sophie muttered.

"Well, of course, but it doesn't mean you don't have an idea."

"I did. I wanted a ballgown. I wanted what you Americans have in the south."

"I don't understand. What about the south?" Addison angled her body to face Sophie more.

"I wanted a southern belle dress. Like in *Gone with the Wind*. Like *Beauty and the Beast*. A big full-sleeved cotillion dress. But when I tried those on, it was…" Sophie scrunched her nose and narrowed her eyes. "*Effroyable!*"

"It couldn't have been that terrible." Addison patted her hand.

Sophie closed her eyes. The memory of the way she felt in the last cotillion-style dress she'd tried on coursed through her mind like Balthazar racing to his first Grand Prix de Paris.

"I'm telling you, it was ghastly. It was a complete disaster. Swallowed in all that fabric, I looked like a sumo wrestler with the oversized satin sleeves puffed up, and the hoop skirt—oh, lord— that looked like it belonged on an Oompa Loompa."

Addison snorted. "Where were the bridal consultants during all this?" she asked.

Sophie gave a nonchalant shrug. "It was peak bridal season, and it was a madhouse. I didn't really expect to need so much help because I had an image in my head of what I wanted. But I was wrong."

"Fair enough." Addison nodded, her lips pursed. "Okay, what else? You have to have given thought to the color, at least."

"I'm not sure pure white looks right on me. It makes me look pasty."

Addison laughed. "Oh, please. You have a beautiful glow to your skin. I'm the one who looks barely alive." She pulled up her sleeve to show alabaster skin appearing to have never been kissed by sunlight.

Sophie giggled. Her friend did look almost like the cartoon ghost—what was his name?—Casper or something?

"Any other requests?"

"I want to be the most beautiful bride ever." Sophie shrugged a single shoulder.

Addison laughed. "Well, that's a given."

"I'm not trying to be a bridezilla."

Addison chuckled.

"Addy, I've been doing this alone. I never established any real friendships here in Paris, outside of those on the farm." She lifted her hands in the air, palms up, and shook them as she spoke. "All those years away in boarding schools. It's been so hard. Marte and Agnes have been great. And Leila, of course, but they are like my *moms*. It's not the same as having my best friend here." Her phone buzzed in her purse, and with a quick glance at the display, Sophie rolled her eyes. "And Claude. Oh, he seems to show such little interest in anything about the wedding."

Addison nodded, tucked her hand into Sophie's, and rested her other hand on top. "Why aren't they here with you today?"

"Honestly, I couldn't handle seeing the disappointment on their faces again. I figured I would keep looking on my own and bring them back later, once I've narrowed it down more."

"Okay. I'm here, and we *will* find your dress."

"I hope so because I'm almost ready to give up." Her eyes welled from the pure frustration planning her wedding had become. It was no longer exciting. A seed had grown inside of her, wishing they had just eloped. Not something she'd ever tell Claude. He'd have rushed her to the nearest courthouse if he had anything to say about it.

Addison's fingers tightened around hers.

"Dress after dress, and there was nothing. No spark." Sophie exhaled loudly. "They didn't feel right. Not like the wow factor I get when I dress up."

Addison nodded. "That's normal."

"It's never been this hard before. I've always been able to find the perfect outfit for any event."

A tight-fitting brilliant cobalt suit stepped up to the front of the couch. The twill fabric almost sparkled under the lights. Sophie blinked and had to strain her neck to find the face of the towering man standing in front of her. Ash-blond hair covered his forehead in a wave. A deep dimple filled each of his cheeks as he smiled.

"*Allô!* I am Alain, your bridal consultant. I am here to make all of your dreams come true." He brought the tips of his fingers to his lips in a noisy kiss before opening his hand in an explosive gesture.

Sophie had noticed him earlier, hovering in the background as they chatted, no doubt waiting for the right moment to introduce himself. It was impossible to miss that suit of his. The way he'd stood off to the side, without interrupting them, yet forcing himself into the scene, he was a perfect example of discretion. She liked him immediately.

"Are we looking for one dress or two?" Addison asked.

"Two dresses?" Sophie asked. She tilted her head to the side and continued looking up at Alain as her bottom lip slipped between her teeth.

Alain chuckled. "Oh yes, that may be what we need. A ceremony dress and a reception dress. It would certainly give us more options to choose from."

"Who does that?" Sophie asked. Her brow creased as she stared up at Alain, then turned to face Addison.

"It's not a new trend, though, of course, it's reserved for the seriously wealthy." Alain lowered his voice as though he betrayed a deep dark secret.

"Well, I have that going for me, at least," Sophie muttered.

"You know what I mean, darling. Most can barely budget for one wedding dress, certainly not two," Alain said.

"I know. I'm just frustrated. This isn't fun anymore." Sophie sighed.

Addison turned to Alain. "Are you up for turning this on its head?"

His infectious grin made the blue suit pop even more. He positively glowed. "What do you have in mind?" he asked.

"We need to start from scratch. Let's focus on fun things much different than what she originally stated. So, I say let's try on everything that is on a mannequin in the store… We'll begin there and see what happens," Addison said.

"*Magnifique.*"

"But I didn't see anything I liked!" Sophie said.

"Exactly. It's different. You need to be open-minded. It's about having fun. Even if we don't find the one today, we will find more about how you feel, how you see yourself in the dress."

"I'm not so sure," Sophie mumbled. She twisted the ring around her finger.

"Do you trust me?" Addison asked.

"*Oui*, always."

"Well, then, I trust Alain to make today enjoyable for us. We can stress about *perfect* later. Today, let's just see you smile." Addison winked at the consultant.

Alain beamed and clapped his hands. "That I can do! Let's start with some champagne, and we can gather some dresses for you."

Sophie's shoulders relaxed, and she crossed her ankles as she leaned against the backrest. With Addison's support and great taste, maybe today wouldn't be completely miserable. Adventures with Addison were always fun.

Her pending nuptials no longer held much excitement. Engaged barely three months, she was already disconsolate about the prospect of planning the event she'd always dreamed of. She sighed.

The only thing keeping me going is Claude. And finally becoming his wife.

She was exhausted. The constant changes and upgrades around the farm had been taxing, to say the least. Claude seemed aloof and contradictory toward her most of the time. And then, the damn nightmare and the overwhelming fear soaking into her bones a little more each time she had it. There was no logical reason for her to be so unhappy. And yet—in many ways—she was, and she couldn't explain it. Even to herself.

"Addy, do you believe in premonitions?"

"Hmm. I'm not sure, I don't think so. I'm more of a tangible, hands-on kind of person. I need to see it to believe it. It's the science nerd in me, I guess. Why do you ask?" Addison asked.

"Oh, nothing, just saw a talk show that had a whole hour about it, and it made me curious. It was dumb. Never mind." Sophie waved her hand in a nonchalant gesture to end the conversation.

She longed to confide in her best friend. And she'd never hesitated about sharing her innermost thoughts with her before, but something held her back. Maybe Addy would dismiss her nightmares as easily as Claude had, and that kind of disappointment would be hard to handle right now. It was best to keep it to herself. Even though deep inside, Sophie hated to battle these fears on her own, instead of sharing with others and getting a better handle on them. The constant unease was tearing her apart from the inside out.

Twenty minutes flashed by as they sat and sipped champagne, chatting about how Addison's sisters were over the moon excited to be participating in Sophie's wedding. While they weren't at all close to Sophie, they had met her many times since Addison's wedding, and since Sophie didn't come from a big family, she was borrowing from her friends.

"I'm sorry Savannah didn't make this trip. She just couldn't take the time away from the office. Her start-up business has her working twelve to fifteen-hour days, lately," Addison said.

Sophie nodded. She knew all about crazy work obligations. Never a fan of math before, being the temporary accountant was enough to make her loathe the subject. She'd become a vet to work with her horses, not pound numbers into a computer.

"I've pulled some fresh looks for you," Alain said as he appeared from behind them. "The first three are from the front of the salon, then I pilfered from other sections."

"Great, so what do you have in store for us?" Addison asked.

"I've chosen ballgowns similar to what Sophie originally described."

"But I told you I looked hideous. Why are you torturing me?" Sophie pouted.

"Like Addison suggested, we put you in them, and you tell us exactly what you like, don't like, and most importantly, how you feel inside the dress. This is where we start," Alain suggested.

Addison bobbed her head so hard it looked like she was at a heavy metal concert instead of a bridal salon. Sophie was sure if she continued, it was going to detach itself from her neck.

"Then, I went in a completely different direction with some fully fitted selections," Alain continued. "Let's get you started, *mademoiselle*." He lifted his shoulders and waved his hands in the air, giving the widest, toothiest smile Sophie had ever seen on a man. Turning on his heel, he practically skipped from the showroom floor.

She followed Alain into a large dressing room where a young woman was standing in the far corner. "This is Monique. She will be helping you with the dresses."

The first dress she tried on was an empire waist, satin ballgown, with a strapless, heart-shaped beaded top cascading down. Standing in the room full of mirrors, she stared at herself and cringed. The ballgown flowed out with fully layered, creased folds of sparkling tulle. The top of the dress was pretty, but the bottom was as big as you could get. Though she couldn't deny it, she appeared the true essence of a princess. Walking out to the waiting area, she stood on the platform and slowly spun around to face Addison.

Sophie patted the area directly below the hem of the bodice. "The ballgown, it's too poufy here. It's too much in all the wrong places…"

"Okay, what do you feel? Not what you see," Addison said.

"Well—"

"No. Close your eyes first. Sense yourself."

"I agree. Don't distract yourself with a visual," Alain suggested.

"It's heavy. The weight of the bottom is pulling

my top down. I just don't feel pretty, and I feel like I'm about to flash my chest," Sophie said. "I'm sorry." Her voice choked up.

"Breathe, sweetheart. There are no wrong answers, Soph. I want to know how you really feel. If you don't feel pretty, there is no way you can walk down the aisle in this dress."

"No. We won't let you," Alain agreed. "You must feel beautiful. In your soul, not just in your eyes."

"But, I don't."

"Shall we burn the dress then?" Addison asked.

Sophie's eyes popped open.

Alain's face drained of color as he stared at her best friend, his expression one of abject horror.

Addison looked from Sophie to Alain, her head swiveling between them as she laughed so hard she snorted and wrapped her arms around her stomach.

Hand over his heart, Alain let out a whoosh of breath. "Ah. A joke? An American funny!"

Sophie groaned. "*Oui*. She has a warped sense of humor, Alain, I warn you now."

Addison nodded, swiping at the tears rolling down her cheeks. "She's not sad anymore, at least." Addison grinned at Alain and shrugged.

He placed his hand over his heart and nodded. "*Touché.*"

Ten minutes later, they re-emerged from the back, and Alain held his hand out to help Sophie back onto the platform.

"This next dress is a full fit and flare with a solid satin bottom," Alain explained to Addison. Facing a three-sided mirror, Sophie took in her reflection. The dress fit her entire body snugly from the top down past her hips, almost too much so. Then, just behind her bottom, it spread out, reminding her of a peacock's rear end. The only breathing room was at the ankles where it flared out. There was no beading, no lace, no decoration at all past the bodice as if they ran out of budget and couldn't finish the dress. Scalloped lace covered the stunning top in a V-shape from below her breasts up to her shoulders, topped in dainty capped sleeves. The beadwork stopped short at the waist, and the bottom was a solid piece of unadorned satin.

In the mirror, Sophie caught Addison's gaze and the small shake of her head. She agreed. This dress was more of a white evening gown meant for the opera than a walk down the aisle to marry her soulmate.

"And that's a no!" the girls said in unison, followed by a fit of giggles.

Alain led Sophie to the back of the store again to try on another dress from his collection.

Twenty minutes later, they reemerged from the back. Standing on the platform again, Sophie faced Addison. "It just doesn't work for me."

"What do you like about it?" Addison asked.

"I love the belt. I like the top, but I'm not sold on the bottom. The lace on the tulle is just not doing it for me." She smoothed her hands against the sides of the skirt.

"I'm not a huge fan of the lacy tulle, either," Alain admitted.

Sophie looked down at the scalloped lace hem and scrunched her nose.

Alain and Addison chuckled at her expression.

"I'm sorry it's so complicated. I'm usually not this hard to dress, or shop for."

"Weddings are complicated. The dress is one of the most important parts of the entire event. If it's wrong, the bride will know it, and the guests will feel it. Nothing else is nearly as vital as the dress. It must be *exquis*," Alain explained.

Sophie nodded. "And to spend so much on a single dress I'll never wear again, it has to be perfect. It has to make me feel as though I could walk on clouds."

"Have you considered a custom order?" Alain asked.

"Of course, but I can't order something if I have no idea what I want."

"Fair enough. Why don't we do this? I have a digital camera—"

"Ugh! To immortalize me looking at my worst. Please, *non*." Sophie buried her face in her hands.

"Sophie, you are a drama queen. And a bridezilla!" Addison narrowed her eyes at her.

She glared at her best friend. The pit of her stomach clenched and churned.

"Listen. Really, it's not a bad idea. We can make a scrapbook out of the pictures. We can put you in the dresses, snap a picture of the entire dress, and then cut out the parts you do like and put those together, and parts you don't like so we'll know what not to bother with in the future. We'll also do it with magazines and add to the scrapbook later."

Alain bobbed his head and flittered about, slipping out of the viewing area and into the back, returning moments later with the camera.

"We should take two pictures. One of the front and one of the back," he suggested.

Sophie shrugged and sucked in a deep breath. Though she hated the idea of seeing images of herself in these dresses, Alain and Addison had a point.

Three hours later, giddy from the champagne in her near-empty stomach, Sophie felt far better about the wedding than she had in months. She still wasn't convinced any of the dresses were the right one, but she no longer dreaded the prospect of it all.

"Can we set aside the last three dresses we all agreed she looked good in, so we can make an appointment to come back with the family?" Addison asked. "In the meantime, we'll compile the scrapbook so we can bring it in, too."

"*Oui*, that is a good idea," Alain said.

"We can also focus on bridesmaid's dresses when we come back. I think we have done enough for today, and we should go spoil ourselves with a high-calorie lunch," Addison said.

CHAPTER 2

Breakfast Bickering

Sophie

The months sped by as Sophie immersed herself in wedding planning and taking a more active role in managing the business aspect of their horse breeding farm, leaving the care of the horses and their breeding in Claude's more-than-capable hands.

With Addison's help, she had ordered a custom-designed dress. Once that was managed, the rest of the preparations came together well.

She was even starting to feel a little more enthusiastic about it all. Her fiancé had not shown much interest, but that was to be expected, right? Her father continually reminded her money was no object. And with a guest list skidding past the eight hundred mark, a large budget was a requirement, not a luxury.

As the sun dipped below the horizon, Sophie turned off the light in her office and headed to the main house for dinner. It had been another long day, and she was exhausted from the dozens of thoughts flitting through her head. A night off to relax with friends and family was just what she needed.

Sophie drew in the aroma of coffee and decadence. Carson, their onsite chef and master miracle worker with all things culinary, had made crepes filled with eggs, cheese, ham, mushrooms, and spinach, covered with a drizzle of hollandaise sauce. Her favorite. As she took a bite, the flavors filled her mouth with pleasure. *Pure heaven.* It had been weeks since she'd sat down for a meal at the farm. It was a nice change of pace to be there first thing in the morning instead of rushing through the city. She loved that Marte always made sure there was plenty of fresh cream on the table for her coffee. The farm's house manager knew her so well.

Her father hadn't joined them as he had other business to attend to, but Claude was there, and she loved having the rare breakfast alone together—especially since he had not spent the night with her again. Sipping her coffee, letting it bring her to life from the inside, she smiled at Claude.

He smiled back. "So, what are your plans this morning?" he asked.

"Noémie and I …"

Claude set his cup in the saucer with a clatter. "Is that all you do? I'm so tired of hearing about the wedding. Every day it's the wedding this … and the wedding that."

Sophie flinched. "But you asked…" She dropped her hands in her lap and strangled the cloth napkin as heat crawled up her neck.

"And I'm sorry I did," he muttered.

Silence descended like a heavy blanket of snow covering a forest. Sophie picked at her breakfast. Her appetite had vanished. A solid block of dread filled her stomach instead.

Claude sat across from her like a statue. The tension in the air was so thick you could slice it like cake. Their wedding was getting closer, and she was beginning to wonder if he was having second thoughts. There was a noticeable disconnect between them. It seemed like he picked fights with her—more often than not—over the smallest details.

He had stopped participating in the meetings, hadn't shown any interest in months. In the beginning, Sophie had tried to get him more involved, to share in the planning. He'd always been too busy with other things. Said the big day was up to her, he would be okay with anything. *Well, that certainly wasn't true.* So, she had accepted it was on her shoulders alone to make it happen.

Well, her and her wedding planners.

Yes, plural.

Papa suggested them after he'd watched her struggle to find a dress and depression had overwhelmed her.

If Claude didn't want to know what she was doing, why did he always ask? Did he honestly think things like this happened in a vacuum? On their own? What did he expect?

Her chest was tight—as if a five-hundred-pound elephant rested on it; her heart ached. Claude was her best friend. One of her only friends and it hurt not to be able to talk to him. To tell him her every thought and feeling about the most significant moment in their lives thus far.

Claude was shutting her out. A feeling of despair invaded every cell. She missed him. Even though he was right next to her, he was a million miles away. He was unreachable in ways she struggled to process.

And he seemed constantly angry with her. Even the slightest thing would set him off and shut him down. The frequency was startling in many ways. It was always her fault. No matter what the topic was, it somehow was turned around, and she was the reason they were fighting, why he was mad.

She longed for the days of the past when they were on the same page. When he was happy to see her and didn't go out of his way to avoid her, full of excuses for his absences. She missed feeling loved. The sense of security she had always felt with him was battered and torn.

Were they making a huge mistake? Was he trying to tell her with his actions instead of words? Should they cancel everything? Claude wasn't a coward by any stretch of the imagination, but the last few months had left her feeling adrift. Unconnected. Unwanted. Utterly alone.

Her heart sank. It was like living through the hell of her chronic nightmares during her waking hours. The tension and anxiety only escalated, making it hard to breathe. Sniffing back tears, she bit her lip until the metallic taste of blood yanked her back, and she turned her attention back to her plate. She refused to cry. The idea of eating nauseated her. She picked up her coffee, hoping to keep her hands steady enough to drink without spilling it all over her cashmere sweater.

The tension between them lasted while they sat at the table, both ignoring their plates.

Claude pushed back his chair and paused, staring at her. "Sophie, I never wanted any of this," he said and stalked out of the dining room. The screen door slapped against the frame as he left the house.

The bereft feeling of his departure beat against her heart as a reminder, maybe they didn't want the same things anymore.

With a sigh, Sophie choked back a sob. Leaning back in her chair, she closed her eyes in a useless attempt to bring back the sense of peace she had before breakfast.

It hadn't worked. Though her fourth cup of coffee had brought her mind to life, at least enough to get some work done, it had done nothing to lift the melancholy that had settled into her soul. Deep within her gut, there was this small fear Claude was telling her he wanted out of their pending nuptials.

Shrugging it off, she knew she was sensitive. If Claude wanted out, he would just say so. *Wouldn't he?*

Well, there was nothing she could do about it

now, but there were plenty of things needing her attention today. The sudden banging and sawing sounds coming from the upper floors announced the workday had begun.

Leaving the table, she headed toward the stable manager's office, located in the barn. She'd been holed up in there while they were tearing apart the bedrooms-turned-offices in the main house. This project had been ongoing for more than two years. Eddie, their stable manager, didn't mind, telling her there was plenty of room for them both, and he'd rather be outside than tied to a desk anyway.

Sophie kicked at the pebbles on the path in front of her. She had no idea what her father was doing up there. He'd banned her from participating, telling her she had enough on her plate, and he'd handle it. She wasn't even allowed upstairs to see the progress. Or if there actually had been any. Seriously, how long did it take to install bookshelves and slap a new coat of paint on the walls?

"What's the big deal?" she muttered, her foot striking a large rock in front of her. "And why can't I at least see what's going on?"

She had felt lost lately. Completely alone. Besides handling the wedding preparations on her own, she was responsible for getting the farm's finances organized and handed off to their new accountant. Then, add the end of the annual horse breeding season, which kept the entire stable staff hopping, as well as extensive renovations to their already burdened shoulders. It was exhausting and overwhelming.

Who knew what her father was thinking? He certainly wasn't confiding his plans with her. Only Claude. The two of them often huddled together, silent whenever she walked into a room.

Ah, well. It was best to leave them to it. She did have more than enough on her plate.

The damn new accounting software was glitchy. And, every chance her father got, he reminded her advanced technology wasn't always better than old-fashioned brainpower. But, you couldn't beat digital file storage or the ability to instantly send drafts of documents via email.

Their oldest and dearest client, Mr. Martin, had finally accepted another colt from them. But it had come with conditions. It was the first sale to him since the unfortunate scandal with the colt, Balthazar. When Mr. Martin first learned his new horse had been drugged, he'd accused them of deception. It had taken a lot to clean up that mess. It still rankled her, their old horse trainer had not faced justice for what he'd done, leaving it an open wound for their family and staff.

Her father had agreed to have Magnus drug tested by an outside doctor before Mr. Martin would take possession of the horse and finalize the purchase. It had taken them almost two years to rebuild their relationship.

So, she really didn't have the time or the energy to deal with Claude's pissiness, or her father's extensive remodeling projects.

After reaching the barn office, Sophie dropped into the chair and took a deep breath. She turned the computer back on and began pulling together the final papers for Magnus. Mr. Martin would come sometime after lunch to pick him up and would expect everything to be in order. More important though, she needed everything to be perfect and above reproach.

CHAPTER 3

Wedding Angst

Claude

C laude Durand leaned against the door jamb and glowered at his fiancée as she once again ignored him while on the phone with a member of the snob squad. That was all she seemed to ever do. Talk to one of them. Email one of them. Meet with one of them. Or all of them, as the case had been the last few months. They were like a gaggle of Guinea keets, always squawking and talking over one another.

He flinched when he heard their names mentioned, and his blood seemed to boil when he heard their voices. It wasn't his fault they'd taken over his whole world and barely left any actual room for him in it.

He knew he'd hurt her feelings at breakfast and had hoped to apologize. But listening to her on the phone irritated him. Again. He stepped back through the office door and headed to his mother's house to check-in.

With a huff, Claude tossed his sweater on the back of the couch as he made his way through the family room and into the kitchen. "Seriously, could it get any more ridiculous?" he grumbled.

"Tsk. Tsk. Stop nagging about the wedding arrangements."

"How do you even know what's on my mind?" He glared at his mother.

"Because, my dear boy, it's all that's on anyone's mind these days."

He groaned. "Why does it have to be this way? Why can't we just have a simple ceremony and be done with it?"

Claude's mother shook her head and lifted her gaze to the ceiling. The look of exasperation on her face was not lost on him. "You didn't choose to marry a simple woman, so why on earth would you expect anything different from her?"

He huffed out another breath.

"Did you pick another fight with Sophie?" she asked.

"*Non.* Not really. It's just that I haven't seen

much of Sophie the last two weeks and hoped to have just a few minutes with her that wasn't all about *that* for a change. She's been flitting around, always surrounded by one of the *fearsome foursome*. I can't even keep up with it all now."

"They are wedding planners, and if you think Sophie has little time for you now, imagine if the *fearsome foursome*, as you call them, didn't handle the bulk of the work." Leila grinned.

Claude rolled his eyes. The entire thing was a spectacle for sure.

"Save your input for where it will matter."

"And where is that, *Maman*?" He slid onto a kitchen chair and folded his hands on the table.

"For the marriage. The wedding is all about the bride. The marriage is about the relationship."

"That's a bit sexist, don't you think? Shouldn't I have a say in how my wedding is put together?" He narrowed his eyes at his mother.

"Sure, if you are on the same page as the bride, or footing the entire bill for the event—otherwise, it's smarter to shut up and look happy." Her eyes crinkled at the edges as she spoke.

"Ugh." Claude dropped his chin to his chest and closed his eyes.

"If you really care, give Sophie some suggestions about what you'd like to see. I know you hate big displays, but do you really hate the whole idea enough to ruin Sophie's happiness? She loves the spotlight and has been chattering about her wedding since she was a little girl."

He groaned. His mother was right. For Sophie, he'd do it. He'd do anything for her. He needed to stop fighting her and start taking an active part of the wedding planning. Claude forced himself to take a deep breath and felt the tension drain out of him.

"Can you stay awhile and visit?" she asked.

"Sure, I'm starving."

"Good, let's have lunch, and you can focus on something other than the wedding for an hour or so." Leila patted his shoulder.

"I would like that. I need a break from all of this."

Lunch with his mother was the perfect remedy to cheer him up. Especially as of late, when the world revolved around wedding details, setup, and changes. Even his mother was unusually distracted by it all.

With the endless construction onsite, he was always tripping over new people, and it was all about the wedding. Everywhere he turned, it was the only topic he heard. All day. Every day. It was like he'd ceased to matter. Ironically, this was precisely why he'd been so slow to propose. He'd been afraid this would happen that their nuptials would turn into a big production, having nothing to do with who he was or what they meant to each other. Which was the last thing he wanted.

On the other hand, if he was honest with himself, it was exactly who Sophie was, and his mother was right. His fiancée had been perfecting her wedding plans since they were children. Every time she played with her dolls, he'd often caught a glimpse of a wedding procession or something similar taking place. It had been her favorite scene to reenact.

"Claude, where are you?"

Shaking his head, he turned his attention back to his mother. Lunch was already set, and she'd put a pitcher of fresh lemonade on the table.

"*Pardon, Maman*. I was distracted. So, besides the wedding, what else is new?" He poured them each a glass of lemonade and took a sip.

Lcila paused for a moment and gave him a searching look before answering. "I've joined a dating website."

Spitting out his drink, he pounded on his chest, gasping for air. He set the glass down hard on the table, and lemonade sloshed down the side.

"Really, Claude." She took a napkin and wiped up the spill.

Finally catching his breath, he stared at his mother through watery eyes. After what had happened with the last guy, he hadn't expected his mother to throw her hat in the ring ever again. She'd been alone most of his life. The only other time she'd considered dating since his father had passed away had been an unmitigated disaster. Where her beau, their old horse trainer, Jacques, turned out to be a fraud and a thief, and almost a murderer—he'd nearly killed Sophie when he'd hit her over the head with a rock and left her unconscious. Claude still hoped to catch up with him in a dark alley one day, since the police had yet to capture him.

"Cat got your tongue?" she asked.

"Hmm. Just surprised is all. Are you sure?" He took a huge bite of his sandwich to stifle his commentary. Are you insane? What about last time? But, ultimately, he was pleased to see the experience hadn't ruined her enthusiasm for romance, after all. "*Non.* I thought I would keep it strictly platonic and friendly and completely online for now."

Swallowing hard, he asked, "What are your plans going forward?"

"A friend from school suggested I focus on no more than five gentlemen at a time."

"Five!" He took a gulp of his lemonade to wash down the sudden drought in his throat.

"*Merde*, Claude, you're a tad melodramatic. I'm not going to be sleeping with them. I won't even be sharing a meal with them."

Eyes wide, he nearly choked on the liquid sliding down his throat. "Okay, sorry. You are right. So, you will be chatting up five men at a time, go on." He lifted his glass in a half salute before bringing it to his lips.

"Well, the idea is to get to know them without it being complicated by social interactions. I would get a chance to learn their minds and see if we even have anything in common long before I have to sit through a meal and hope they can chew without their mouth hanging wide open." She grinned.

Claude chuckled at the image of a slack-jawed old man sitting across from his mother. "So, what happens if you decide you don't have enough in common?"

"Then, I move on to a different person and start over."

"Sounds exhausting."

"It's been kind of fun so far. I've been talking to two men for about a week now."

He nodded and took his last bite of sandwich. "That's good. And what about meeting them?"

"I think I'll wait until I've gotten to know them for at least six months. I'm in no rush. See how lucky you are to be getting married and settling down? No more dating or trying to find love." She'd maneuvered his bad mood around to bite him in the behind—the glint in her eye was classic Leila.

"*Oui,* I'm a very lucky man," he muttered. Suddenly uncomfortable with the direction of their conversation, he hoped for an easy escape.

She reached out and squeezed his hand. "You really are. Now, stop pouting and go steal a kiss from that pretty girl of yours. I'm sure it will lift your sour mood."

"I think I'll do just that." He scooted from his chair, kissed his mom's cheek, and strode through the family room to grab his sweater.

Leila called out as he reached the door. "Good luck."

"Thanks for lunch." He waved back at her as he headed out in search of Sophie.

Hands stuffed in his pockets, he headed for the barn where he expected Sophie to still be holed up. The walk across the property cleared his head, and the slight breeze against his face was welcome.

Lunch with his mother had put things into perspective. At least he wasn't as frustrated as before.

Admittedly, he'd been in a foul mood—lashing out at those around him. The wedding preparations had taken their toll on his typically good nature, and he hated how disconnected he felt. Especially from Sophie. She was busier than ever, and he expected in the coming week when distant guests began arriving, he'd see even less of her.

A part of him knew it was almost over. It was the last sixteen months of planning and nothing else that had left him frustrated and emotionally drained of any interest in the wedding.

It wasn't that he wasn't busy. There was the construction of the offices in the house, the unlimited new projects around the farm. The entire property was undergoing updates. Some structural, like the offices in the main house, others merely cosmetic like painting and landscaping, and their breeding season was just winding down.

Their season started with the colts. Zorro, Magnus, Tornado, Saragon, and Goliath had all inseminated the chosen mares and were now being sent to their new owners. Magnus was the last to leave because of the added stipulations Mr. Martin's stables had put on them before agreeing to the sale.

The farm was always so quiet after the colts left. The attention shifted to the mares remaining.

Morningstar and Twilight had already birthed their foals. A stunning filly they named Duchess, and a colt they'd dubbed Sultan because it suited his personality. They were already in the back paddock. Now they waited on Jezebel's foal to wind things down for the season.

They had intentionally planned the inseminations to be staggered so they could give more attention to each horse. Also to prevent stretching out their resources, with everyone handling multiple births as well as the wedding. Sophie had charted the schedule in precise detail to make sure no one, including the horses, would be unnecessarily stressed. She even admitted to having concerns about mistakes being made if anyone was distracted.

Claude bet the nefarious dealings of Jacques, with the illegal collection and sale of semen from the stable's prized colts, had played into her concerns. It had affected the entire organization, shocking everyone to learn they'd been betrayed by one of their own. If the staff wasn't overburdened, they could keep their eyes open for anything amiss and stop it long before things reached a critical level.

Pausing at the closed door to take in a deep breath, he popped his head in Sophie's office. "I think Jezie's foal will make its appearance tonight. Want to join me?"

Sophie glanced up from the file in her hand and smiled. It lit up her face and made his breath hitch. He loved it when she looked at him as though he was all that mattered in the world. It wasn't very often these days, so this smile made the demons chasing him slink away.

"I'd love to. Why don't you give me another hour to finish up this paperwork, and then I can meet you in the stables?"

"That should be fine. I've got some things to do in the meantime, so come by when you're free. Love you."

"Love you, too."

Claude wanted to touch her, to kiss her, wrap his hands around her and hold her tight, but he needed to make it up to her first. He slipped out of her office with a grin as wide as his face. Playing it right, he might woo Sophie a little before Jezie needed them. Heading to the main house, he hoped to enlist Marte's assistance in his scheme. A romantic at heart, she'd always been the one to help him smooth things over with Sophie. He crossed his fingers Marte would be up for this challenge.

Entering the kitchen, he saw Carson at the stove, as usual, creating another fantastic meal for the staff.

"*Allô!*" Carson turned to face Claude. "How are you today?"

"Things are great. It looks like we may have our last foal soon."

"Good, good. What can I get for you?" Carson asked.

"I was hoping to pick Marte's brain about a surprise for Sophie tonight."

"Ah, an intimate rendezvous." Carson waved his wooden spoon in the air like a magic wand.

"Exactly." Claude laughed.

"What are you thinking? Maybe a candlelight dinner for two in her office?" Carson smiled.

"A bit less formal and a little more practical?"

"*Je ne comprends pas?*"

"I'm thinking more along the lines of a small picnic in the stables, so we can keep an eye on Jezebel tonight," Claude said.

"*Magnifique!* I have the perfect solution."

Marte entered the kitchen from the back stairs just as Carson whipped around to stick the wooden spoon back into the enormous stainless-steel stockpot on the stove.

"And what are your plans for this evening,

monsieur? Are you planning to join the staff for dinner?" Marte asked Claude.

"*Non, non.* Not while there is love in the air." Carson chuckled.

Marte turned her inquisitive gaze toward Claude, her perfectly plucked brow arched.

He grinned and winked with a twinkle in his eye. "I am planning dinner with Sophie tonight."

"Ah, then, of course, we shall help," Marte said.

"I have a big pot of lobster bisque simmering on the cooktop that will ward off the chill, and fresh baguettes in the oven."

"*Merci.*" With a nod, Claude went upstairs to check on the progress of the offices while Marte and Carson worked their magic.

CHAPTER 4

New Beginnings

Sophie

Sophie smiled as the door closed behind Claude. It was good to see him in better spirits, and her heart was light again. She hated when they weren't on the same page about something. It didn't matter what. It sucked big time. At least now, it appeared their argument wouldn't lead to days or weeks of not speaking to one another as so many of them had in the past.

She was grateful he'd reminded her about Jezebel's foal. Though they expected it this week, babies came when babies were ready, never based on a date circled on a calendar, regardless of species. She'd missed Duchess's entrance into the world. By the time she'd made it down to the stables, Morningstar had birthed her foal, and Duchess was already scrambling to walk. She hadn't even been on the farm when Sultan was born. It was a dress-fitting day, so she'd been in the city. Missing them had left an ache in her heart.

Determined not to miss Jezebel's delivery, she'd rescheduled all her wedding appointments so she could be on the farm for the whole week. This just meant more phone calls with her wedding planners to make sure things kept moving while she was busy with the horses. The stress of all that happened the previous year at the farm had left lingering insecurity. First Jacques betrayal and the way he'd attacked her, followed by the loss of two of the foals that season. It had shaken her confidence to the core.

Turning her attention back to the accounting program, she typed in a few commands before it stopped responding, and the screen turned blue.

"Damn it!" Sophie muttered at the frozen computer screen. She was perfectly aware she was doing something wrong, she just didn't have the foggiest idea what the hell it was.

Rebooting the system was the only option. Damn it all to hell. "Stupid ancient technology. It never works when you need it to." She slapped the side of the bulky monitor as though it could understand her before hitting the power button off and on again. Tapping the pen against the desk, she waited for the computer to go through the agonizingly slow process of coming back on.

There was a niggling suspicion the new software wasn't liking the outdated hardware. Sophie hated this old dinosaur of a computer. It had to be at least twenty years old, but her father was adamant about not getting a new system. He'd relented about purchasing the new software because they had hired Tyler to replace their retired accountant but dug his heels in about new equipment for the farm. No doubt, he didn't want to learn a new computer, but it was unlike him to be so adamant about none of the computers being upgraded at all.

This certainly qualified as an intentional infliction of emotional distress. Sophie heaved a healthy sigh. Oh well, she would make it work. *Somehow.*

Logging back into the accounting program, she waited for Tyler to call her back. He was in the city taking a crash course in the software, so he'd be more adept at its idiosyncrasies when he came on board as a full-time accountant. She was looking forward to the day because it was one less thing to manage. She was determined, while it was her domain, she'd update the process enough to make it more manageable than the current system. Thus, if she had to manage it again, it wouldn't be such a nightmare to clean up.

Sophie had loved their last accountant. Amié had been with their farm since the very beginning. But the woman was almost as much of a dinosaur as the damn computer on the desk. And her columnar booklet had been written in a shorthand that wasn't easily translatable. It looked closer to hieroglyphics than anything in French or English.

When she retired earlier in the year, Sophie had been given little choice but to take over after her departure. Of course, at the time, Sophie didn't have any idea what she had agreed to take on, and she regretted it almost daily.

The jangling of the phone brought her out of her meandering thoughts and back to reality. The voice on the other end brought a reluctant smile to her lips.

"Tyler, glad you called me back. Please tell me you understand what they are teaching you over there."

His laugh made her feel less anxious about what they were doing.

Twenty minutes later, she understood why it wasn't working. Her determination to bring the farm into the twenty-first century and the digital age was strong. *And I won't be stopped by a damn archaic system even if it kills me.* Sophie glared at the computer, willing it to argue.

Shaking her head, she had to admit things didn't bode well if she was fighting with an old computer as though there was a legitimate battle between them.

But damn it all to hell and back, she wanted to be outside with Claude and Eddie and the horses, not locked in an office out of everyone's way doing grunt work instead. And that wouldn't happen until she'd taken care of the accounting mess in front of her.

Feeling good about the day's work, she logged out of the computer and put the files scattered on her desk away looking forward to seeing Claude and the horses.

CHAPTER 5

Life Interrupts

Claude

C laude stretched the heavy wool blanket out in the stall next to Jezebel's to cushion them from the rough straw scattered throughout the small space. He paused a moment to listen to her pacing around. As she walked, he noticed her slow gait. She was restless, another sure sign her time was approaching, and things would be progressing soon. He folded and draped another blanket, a much softer chenille, across the door.

Blood hummed in his veins. He felt like a nervous schoolboy with a crush planning his first date. Not a man whose nuptials were fast approaching. He'd spent most of his life fearing

Sophie'd figure out he was a fraud and she deserved so much more than he could ever give her, and run screaming for the hills. His stomach churned at the idea of losing her. Even after putting a ring on her finger, the self-doubt lingered.

Being at odds with Sophie regularly had been hard on them, but his short temper with her was on him. She was doing what she was supposed to, and instead of supporting her, he'd basically shut her out and all talk of their future. Tonight, he aimed to change that. Maybe fix the rift between them. He had to try. Wringing his hands, his gut clenched as he thought of how his attitude pushed her away—only to get angrier at her for the distance between them.

An oversized wicker basket rested in the corner. A thermos of bisque nestled at the bottom, and a bottle of Louis Jadot and glasses tucked beside it. Fresh bread and warm Brie arranged artfully on a plate, wrapped in plastic, sat on the lid of the basket. After a quick glance, everything appeared perfect, so he stepped out to check on Jezebel.

"Hey, girl." Claude rested his cheek on her forehead. A soft neigh came from the horse. "Soon, sweetheart, you'll be a mother."

He patted her neck. The horse bobbed its head.

"Are you flirting with Jezie again?" Sophie asked, stepping up behind him.

"Guilty." Claude chuckled. "How is the world of finance going?" He turned around and embraced her.

"Fine. It's a lot of work, but I think Tyler will be a great asset. He's pretty intuitive."

Claude smiled and kissed her nose. He would wait to ask about the wedding plans. What he wanted—*no, needed*—was a few moments all about them and not the circus surrounding them.

He maneuvered them closer to Jezebel, and the horse nipped at his hair.

Sophie giggled. "She wants your attention."

With an exaggerated sigh, he turned his head, and Jezebel blew in his ear. "Yup, my charms are in high demand."

She laughed and stroked Jezebel's neck.

Taking her hand, Claude led Sophie to the next stall. As he opened the gate, Sophie stepped inside, turned around, and kissed him.

Kicking off her ankle-high rubber rain boots, she sat down on the blanket and smoothed out the spot beside her. "This is so sweet. I love it." Her eyes brightened, and as she gazed back up at him, her cheeks flushed.

Claude slipped the blanket from the gate before

joining her in the stall. Covering her legs, he sat beside her and leaned against the back wall. He opened the wine and poured them each a glass before bending over and kissing her neck.

Humming, Sophie rested against him and snuggled. He pulled the blanket to stretch across his lap as well and wrapped an arm around her, holding her tighter. It felt good to be together without distractions. The plate of Brie and bread was devoured as the wine relaxed them. They sipped the burgundy as their shared body heat kept them comfortable against the slight chill in the air.

"I've been thinking about the wedding," Claude said.

There was a whoosh of breath as Sophie inhaled and tensed in his arms. It stung. He had done this to her. He had turned her dreams into something less magical than they should have been. Shame flooded through him.

"I'm sorry," he whispered. "I haven't been supportive lately. And I know I haven't been involved at all."

"It's okay," she said in a low voice, taking a gulp of her wine.

He kissed the back of her hair. "*Non*, it's not. I've been a jerk. I told you I was okay with whatever you wanted, then I didn't want to hear about the things you were doing to make those plans a reality."

"Why? Why did you push me away and not want to hear anything? I've been terrified you've been having second thoughts." Sophie's voice was muffled, and the vibrations in her shoulders told him she was crying.

Flabbergasted, Claude asked, "About marrying you?"

"*Oui.*"

The air in his lungs escaped, leaving the sensation of ice in his chest. "Oh, Sophie!" He set his glass down and turned her in his arms so he could see her face. His thumb caught the single tear escaping. Pulling her tight against his chest, resting her head on his breastbone, he stroked her hair.

"I'm sorry you doubted my love. There has never been a day I wasn't sure about you. About us. Or what I feel for you." He continued to stroke her hair, his lips whispering against the top of her head tucked under his chin.

Sophie relaxed into his arms, letting him hold her closer.

"I've been jealous. And insecure. Truth be told, frustrated at everything going on. It's been over the top."

"The wedding?"

"*Oui*, everything has been about the wedding. The renovations in the main house I understand, but the constant work around the farm I don't. It's just been too much. It's been overwhelming."

"Not everything. I have no idea what Papa is doing to the house. It has nothing to do with the wedding, though. Of that, I'm certain."

"Then why all the craziness with updating the grounds?"

Sophie shrugged. "When it all started, I thought it was to clear out the old rooms and create more office space on the second floor for us, and he was to move his office upstairs to the third floor. But I have not seen the progress. I haven't been allowed on the upper floors in more than a year. Papa said it was to be a surprise."

"The new offices are nice, don't get me wrong, but why the sudden need for so many changes to the rest of the property?" he asked.

"I wonder if Papa is getting all nostalgic because we are getting married. And I'll be leaving home. He hasn't said anything to me about it."

"Well, the progress has been remarkable, and the changes stunning. Bertrand's office on the third floor seems to be taking the most work. They are building bookshelves into the walls. The floors have been sanded and stained. They even added additional windows and private *toilettes*. It no longer looks like a dusty attic."

"That is good to hear. Sounds like it will be a lovely space to work in when renovations are done."

"That's the idea. So anyway, back to the wedding," Claude said.

Sophie's shoulders stiffened. "Not tonight, please. I don't want to fight."

"I agree. No fighting. I would like to offer a suggestion, if I may?"

She turned her head to look him in the eye. He kissed her nose, making her lips turn up into a smile, his following right behind.

"I think I would like a little bit of simplicity added to our ceremony."

"*S'il vous plaît, expliquez.*"

"What I mean is beside all the glitz and glamour I'm sure is involved in spades, I would like a few things special to us, representing us. I don't think ice sculptures and flashing lights do that."

"I have no plans for flashing lights."

He looked down his nose at her. "You know very well what I mean. I would like to have a few simple touches that speak about us."

"*Très bien.* What do you have in mind?"

"We could start with the flowers."

"Floral arrangements? You are concerned about those?" Sophie's expression was skeptical.

"Not concerned. I have a small request. That is all." He held his thumb and forefinger up, showing an inch of space between.

Sophie narrowed her eyes at him but nodded.

"I would like to have forget-me-nots included."

"In the decorations?"

"Everywhere if possible, even in your bouquet. They're our flowers. I think they should be represented."

Sophie kissed him under his chin. "That is easy enough. Any others?"

"Toss out the top hats? Please don't make me wear one. I loathe them."

"Since you asked so nicely, I will cancel the hats." Sophie giggled.

"*Merci.*"

"Any other requests?"

Claude's eyebrow rose. "I'm sure I'll think of something else." He shifted her body to raise her up. Bringing his lips to hers, slow and soft. Her response was enthusiastic, taking it to a new level. She pulled him with her as she leaned back from the sitting position, her back flat on the blanket beneath them.

Their embrace became more passionate as she

tugged at his sweater. Their lips broke briefly so he could pull it over his head. He brushed his lips across her jaw and down her neck, stopping in the center directly above the first button of her silk blouse. He loved how her breath hitched. With slow and deliberate movements, he released the top button. Opening the gap wider, he slid his tongue across her where the button had once rested. She shivered under his touch. He opened a second button and did the same. By the time he had reached the last button, he had reached her navel and she trembled beneath him.

His heart raced as he laid her shirt open on each side, baring her bra and midriff. Her breath hitched as he nipped her skin on his way back up to her neck and captured her lips in a searing kiss.

God I've missed her. I really am the luckiest of men.

Sophie's hands trailed down his back, nails slowly gliding over his skin, causing heat to rise in his core. Her fingers nimbly opened the snap of his jeans. Then, she tucked her hands down the back and cupped his ass.

Claude slipped his thumbs below the waistline of her trousers. With a little tug, he lowered them below her hip bones. He took his time caressing this newly exposed skin. Her body arched under his fingers.

Sophie stretched, bringing her hands to his head, running her fingers through his hair, exposing her breasts as her shirt slid down her sides and the silk fabric pooled under her ribs. She nipped his ear, making his erection pulsate, demanding the barriers between them be removed. Her lips returned to his, and their tongues did a slow sensual mating dance that left him craving more.

His cock throbbed, pressing against his zipper almost painfully. It had been weeks since they had been intimate. He had missed this connection with her. The way their bodies synced with each other as they made love.

Hearing labored breathing coming from Jezebel's stall, he lifted his head and put his finger to her lips. With a sigh caught in his throat, he glanced down at Sophie, and she nodded. The spell was broken. Without words, they moved in unison. Quickly righting their disheveled clothing, they stood and slipped their boots on, and she followed him out of the stall.

Jezebel was on her side, curled up in the straw, struggling to rise. After she lumbered to her feet, she paced the small area in a clockwise circle. Her head came over the stall door, and Claude stroked her neck. Her coat was warm and sweaty as though she'd just had a run around the paddock.

"You're doing good, girl. Any time now."

The horse snorted and continued her trek around the stall before stopping abruptly and lying back down. Sophie leaned against the stall door and peered down at Jezebel as Claude stepped inside.

Moving in measured steps to not spook her, Claude walked around the horse, keeping eye contact and murmuring gentle encouragement. As he neared her back, he wasn't surprised to see a tiny hoof peeking out from under her tail.

"Is she ready then?"

"Any moment now."

"Be right back!" Sophie called out to him as she sprinted from the stables.

Claude continued to croon to the horse, telling her how well she was doing, and that it was almost over. Sophie leaving was an unexpected development, but he could handle the birthing on his own. He was just here as a glorified cheerleader as it was Jezebel doing all the work.

The movement hadn't progressed. There still only the tip of the first hoof extending out, so Claude continued to monitor Jezebel's breathing for any signs of distress. She appeared to be okay. The foal was just taking its sweet time coming into the world.

The crunching of the gravel and straw caught

his attention. Looking up, he saw, Eddie standing with his arms resting on the gate, peering down at them, as Sophie rushed in. She handed a video camera to Eddie and joined Claude in the stall. Taking slow steps, she moved to his side. He immediately noticed she had changed her silk blouse into a more practical sweater. Her rushing out made perfect sense now. In order to help, her arms needed to be less restricted than the silk blouse would have allowed.

During his morning rounds, he'd braided and wrapped Jezebel's tail to prepare for the birth. They'd learned the hard way years ago that it made cleaning the mares up after birthing much easier.

The second hoof slid next to the first, both extending farther out, and then the long muzzle followed. Sophie began crooning to Jezebel and stroking her back as the rest of the foal emerged. And just like that, Jezebel was a new mother. Her beautiful filly lay on the straw.

Claude and Sophie exchanged a smile, caught up in the magic of the moment. The awe on Sophie's face warmed his heart. No matter how many horses they birthed at the farm, each new foal was a precious gift. This was the first time they had been able to share in the experience since becoming full-fledged veterinarians, making the moment even more special. Sophie didn't get to spend nearly as much time with the horses now that she was managing the daily operations of the business end. The beginning of the breeding season was the only time she had the opportunity to really do what she loved the most. While he managed the daily duties of the horse side, together, they handled the farm's breeding and birthing program.

Jezebel ambled to her feet then turned around to nose her new addition. The filly lifted its head and faced her mother. Claude noticed Eddie continued to stand at the edge of the stall, filming the event. Giving Eddie a smile and nod, he turned his attention back to the new mama and foal. The filly stretched its neck and rubbed its face against her attentive mother before pushing her legs in front of her and attempting to stand. Her legs wobbled and folded back to the ground. Jezebel lay back down next to her filly giving silent encouragement. She continued to clean her offspring—to help stimulate breathing and blood flow—as they waited for her to find her land legs.

After a few aborted attempts, the filly stood and took her first steps. Sophie wiped a tear and sighed as she slowly made her way out of the stall.

Watching Sophie out of the corner of his eye, Claude gave a silent thanks to the heavens. Both horses were fine. He didn't think Sophie could bear to lose another so soon. While a loss was part of life, the year before had been rife with multiple still-births and a set of twins not making it, taking the mare with them. Sophie had taken it personally. As if it was her fault the animals had not survived. Having her here with him, and everything going so smoothly, it felt like tonight's birth was a good omen of things to come.

CHAPTER 6

Final Preparations

Sophie

T he house was finally quiet. Though Sophie knew the silence would be fleeting, she was grateful, nonetheless. Having Addison in France early to help with the last-minute wedding preparations, including her two children and Sergei—her husband—had Sophie over the moon. The support of her best friend was everything she needed right now. Although, it had become increasingly clear bringing Addison's entire extended family over so soon was more of a burden than a blessing. Her sisters were sweet enough, especially the youngest two, but Addison's mother, Tandy, defined exasperating.

Sitting in the parlor sipping a much-needed

martini, Sophie rolled her eyes at Addison. "Can't I send them home and only bring them back on the day of the wedding? At least *her*." Sophie said the last word in a low whisper, sneaking a quick glance at the open door.

"I wish." Addison pursed her lips, though there was a mischievous glint in her eye.

"I don't think I can handle a whole week of your mother."

Addison shook her head. "I warned you bringing her over so early was not wise."

"Ugh, I know. I was trying to be practical. I needed the girls here for their final fittings, and it made more sense to bring your family over first then send the plane to Russia for Sergei's. It's a good thing I love you more because his family would have been much better long-term guests." She caught Addison's gaze and gave her a wide, toothy grin.

Addison responded with a slight nod, and, with her attention on the open door, she said, "Yeah, well, now you have to live with her for the week."

Sophie let out an exaggerated sigh. "Seriously, though, what's your secret?"

"Not living in the same house, mostly." Addison shrugged.

"Understood. *Merde.*" Sophie waved a hand in the air giving her words more emphasis.

"She's jealous of your wealth and feels you flaunt it at us peasants." Addison's voice dropped.

Sophie rolled her eyes. "Really?"

Addison's expression deadpanned. "Oh, I'm serious. We were subjected to her rant the entire way over in your private plane."

"I should have made her fly commercial," Sophie grumbled. "Did you explain to her that the costs of flying the four of you, plus her, your four sisters and Savannah's husband to France would be astronomical in commercial? Even if we put you all in the cargo hold!"

Addison choked. "Oh, that's just mean."

Sophie grinned wickedly and gave a little nonchalant half-shrug.

"I did. It didn't help much. Her mind is made up already," Addison said.

"Well, I'm sorry to hear that. Because Tandy is going to really hate me when she sees the wedding."

"I have no doubt." Addison took a sip of her martini.

"I kinda went a little overboard. Can you believe Papa hired four wedding planners!" Sophie let out an exaggerated sigh.

Addison bobbed her head. "Yes. For you, I'm sure even that was cutting it close!"

Sophie swatted at her playfully.

"What's Claude's opinion of your Disney Princess wedding?"

"Disney Princess?" she asked.

"You know, over the top… Full-on fairytale style," Addison said.

"Ah. Well, he's not jealous. That's for sure." Sophie groaned.

"I take it he's not pleased?"

"Claude would have preferred the two of us alone, barefoot on a beach."

Addison placed a hand on her heart, her face filled with mock horror. "It's like he's never met you!"

Sophie rolled her eyes. "*Exactement*! No one who really knows me would ever expect me to be so low-key. Especially for my first wedding."

Addison snorted. "First? Are you planning others?"

"You know what I mean. If this was my third or fourth wedding? Sure, a small, quiet, private event would be understandable and acceptable. But for my first wedding, to my long-term beau? I've waited more than twenty years for this moment." Sophie shook her head. "Low-key was never on the table."

"Yes, well, weddings never were about the groom. They only need to show up on time." Addison grinned.

"Exactly. Not that Claude agrees with that, either."

"What do you mean?" Addison asked as her husband came in. She lifted her face for a kiss as he walked by.

"What are you ladies gossiping about now?" Sergei asked.

"The usual. What's Mama doing?"

Sergei leaned in and kissed her cheek before plopping into an open chair. "Tandy and your sisters are playing with the kids at the moment, but she did ask when dinner would be."

Addison gave Sophie a pointed look.

"We'll make it an early one for her. Or she can eat with the younger kids, and we can go out on the town." Sophie smirked.

"If you plan on going out, I assure you she would expect to be invited."

"We'll do whatever suits you and Sergei."

"It's not about us, love."

"It is for me." Sophie's eyes narrowed.

Addison sighed.

Sophie took a deep breath. This wasn't the hill she'd choose to die on. She would just let it go and hope Addison's mother would be less needy for the rest of her stay. But that woman was an energy vampire. While Addison's roommate in Russia, Sophie had gotten a small taste of Tandy's dramatics, and again later, while in America for Addison's wedding. She'd seen firsthand how controlling Tandy actually was.

Watching Tandy and Addison made her realize how lucky she had been to have the mother she'd had. She missed her *maman*, especially with all the wedding chaos. Her loving guidance and unwavering support were much needed these days as the final details were slowly put in place.

"Will your father and Cassie still arrive at the end of the week?" Sophie asked.

"Yes, they will be here for the wedding, and then plan to stay for the week after to enjoy Paris."

"Why didn't they want to fly over with you?" Sophie asked.

Sergei snorted, and Addison tilted her head and stared at her with an incredulous expression.

"*Your mother*, of course. That would have been an extremely long flight with the three of them on board."

Addison scrunched her nose.

"You have no idea," Sergei said. He directed his gaze to the ceiling.

"Well, nevertheless, I'm glad they're coming," Sophie said.

"I am, too. And since they will be staying in a rental across the Seine, there will be minimal interaction with my mother."

"You are still planning to stay for a few days after the wedding, correct?" Sophie asked.

"Yes, I'll see my mother and sisters off, then I wanted to see you off on your honeymoon before spending a couple of days with Cassie and my father in the city. Sergei's family will be staying in a house next to theirs."

"A little family reunion in Paris. I love it."

"Yes, I'll be so exhausted from all the family time I'll need to go back to work to recover from my vacation," Sergei said and chuckled.

Addison nodded with a grin.

"Well, we should probably figure out supper soon. I suggest we go out and be done with it. I'm sure Papa won't mind," Sophie said.

"Okay, I'll let my mother and sisters know. I think we should leave the children here tonight to make it easier."

"If we must," Sophie grumbled. "I'd still prefer their company to some others."

Addison left the room, heels clicking on the marble floor as she headed to the stairs.

But Sergei's wink and the low rumble in his chest made Sophie giggle.

CHAPTER 7

A Fitting to Remember

Sophie

S ophie glanced over at Addison's four sisters standing in front of mirrors lining the walls of the salon, each getting their dresses fitted. She caught the oldest sister, Savannah's eye, as she turned her head, ignoring the little sarcastic jabs directed by their mother. Tandy fretted over her two youngest, as well as Addison's daughter, Natalya, who was the flower girl.

A hint of another headache crept behind Sophie's eyes. Pushing away thoughts of Tandy, Sophie focused on her dearest friend standing before her. "So, what do you think?" Sophie asked. "Is it the right balance? I wanted the colors to make a statement, but I didn't want to bellow it from the rooftops."

Addison smoothed her hands down her dress and met her gaze. "Sophie, I think the dresses are perfect. They are neutral colors, so they couldn't shout from the roof even if they tried. The different styles really do suit each of us, and the shantung and chiffon fabrics make them not only comfortable but easily managed. So we won't look like a mess in pictures. You've captured the essence of practicality and beauty." Addison squeezed her hand and then glanced over at her sisters. "Thank you for including them, they are so excited to be a part of a celebrity wedding."

"I'm not a celebrity…"

"The girls think you are. They have felt like princesses. It's a whole new world for them. One they don't expect to ever experience again."

One of the wedding consultants walked over with the lead seamstress. "Is *Mademoiselle* pleased with the bridesmaid dresses?"

"*Oui*, they are lovely. *Merci*."

"*Tres bien*. Now, let us get you into yours to see what must be done."

Sophie nodded and followed the woman to the back of the salon. She had been going through the motions the last few weeks until Addison had arrived and put life back in the events.

Twenty minutes later, they returned to the main salon, and she was on display in the center of the room.

Sophie stared at herself in the mirror. The dark circles under her eyes betrayed the baggage she was carrying. Another sleepless night full of the dreaded dreams had left its mark on her. There was never anyone or anything in them, nothing to explain their presence. First, a darkness overwhelmed her, then a feeling of being in a floatation tank. The drop in her stomach after leaving her feeling weightless always wrenched her back into the real world. She still couldn't fathom why these nightmares continued plaguing her. The attempt to hide the evidence under makeup had been an epic failure. The purple hue refused to be tamed, but there was nothing she could do about her appearance. She narrowed her eyes and turned her head away from her reflection.

It was the second-to-the-last fitting for their dresses, to double- and triple-check everything in time to make any major changes.

The wedding was less than a week away. Close to two years of planning had been invested in making her dreams come true. The wedding would be the social event of the season, with more than eight hundred invited guests confirmed.

Sophie stood on the raised platform, surrounded by floor-to-ceiling mirrors. Everyone else was back in their street clothes. Sophie's mother figures, the house managers at the farm and her father's apartment, Marte and Agnes, sat beside Addison and her soon-to-be mother-in-law Leila. Addison's sisters and mother sat with the little ones on the benches on the other side of the salon facing her.

There was an audible gasp from Addison's youngest sisters as she slowly turned in a circle, glancing over her shoulder to get a glimpse of the back of the dress. Marte and Agnes beamed at her, their hands over their hearts, and Leila had tears in her eyes.

Bathed in bright white light under the warm fluorescent bulbs, the crystal beads and small pearls sparkled against her skin. The waist was a little loose, pulling the dress down more than she was comfortable with. Before she could mention it, there was clucking from behind her and hands pulled on each side, tightening it and adding wooden pinch clamps to the loose fabric. She yanked on the top of the dress to put it back in the right position.

"We will continue to work on the size until the very end *mademoiselle*, in case you lose more weight."

Glancing down, there was a knowing look in the woman's eye. Sophie sighed. She wasn't trying to lose weight. It wasn't a vain attempt at glamour. More like the result of too much stress. Things at the stables had been hectic over the last few months. There were more than enough balls to juggle, on top of all the wedding details her various wedding planners couldn't seem to manage without her input. She was desperately looking forward to the honeymoon.

The entire thing was more work than she'd ever considered possible. It was emotional, tense, and fraught with complications and drama. She could almost understand Claude's reluctance at having such an event, not that she would ever admit it out loud. She'd go to her grave first. But in her heart of hearts, she'd longed for this day her entire life. To skip or scrimp on those dreams would only haunt her in the long run.

Turning her attention back to the mirrors, her heart lifted. Even with the corset not fitting snug against her frame—though pulled as tight as the laces would allow and clamped against her tightly— the dress flowed down her body like a waterfall. The crystals sewn into the bodice positively glowed and glittered under the lights. The bottom, though, was a bit long and pooled at her feet, even with four-inch heels on.

More hands tucked the hem under and pinned it, while pulling the rest out to show its length, allowing it to circle around and behind her in a small train. She adjusted her veil, letting it glide over her shoulders. It wasn't a long one, just a short decorative piece attached to a delicate tiara for the ceremony.

As she concentrated on the women pinning her dress in various places, a familiar voice startled her. The friendly tone filled her with warmth.

"*Magnifique*! I believe every woman shall be envious, and every man's head will turn. All eyes will be riveted on you as you glide by on your personal cloud."

She had not seen Alain the last few visits to the salon, and he hadn't been in when they arrived, so having him standing there beside her was unexpected.

The managing bridal consultant wore a startling eggplant blazer that could make one's eyes bleed if they stared at it too long.

Catching Tandy's disdainful expression through one of the side mirrors, Sophie grinned wide, stepped down next to Alain, and enveloped him in an embrace.

"*Merci beaucoup*. It is fabulous, more than I could have imagined," she gushed while holding tight.

"So, you are pleased?" Alain asked as she released him.

"*Oui*, I think we got it right," she said.

"I'd say so. You look *très* beautiful. Perfectly *equise*."

"Ah, *tu es charmant* as always."

Alain preened and grinned, clearly pleased with himself.

"A total one hundred eighty degrees from what I pictured myself in. I hope Claude loves it as much as I do."

Alain gave an exaggerated bow.

Lifting the hem to avoid stepping on it, she made another full circle and sighed. It may have taken longer than expected, and included more drama than necessary, but in the end, standing in front of the wall of mirrors, it had all been worth the effort. She found herself transformed before her own eyes into the princess she'd dreamed of.

Catching Addison's eye, they shared a smile. Addison gave her a thumbs up.

This is it. This is perfect.

CHAPTER 8

Moving Up

Claude

C laude sat at the table, picking at his quiche. It was a rare event to be summoned by Bertrand to breakfast at the farm. A quick glance across the table at Sophie's tight shoulders confirmed she was just as anxious.

His mother sat beside him, oblivious to the tension as she chatted with their guests and their children. Sophie was engrossed in a conversation with Addison, the two as thick as thieves.

Bertrand had yet to tell them what was on his mind. He'd been unusually silent throughout the meal and, frankly, it was grating on Claude's last raw nerve.

Their wedding was in a few days, and there was

so much action on the farm. With the crew cleaning up their construction debris scattered all over the place, he didn't have time for dilly-dallying. As if the year-long remodel project hadn't been stressful enough, supervising the removal of the massive mess left behind was even worse.

Not only were they removing construction debris, but they were also tripping over the vendors setting up for the wedding itself. He was so tired of the endless parade of people and changes. All Claude wanted to do was get back to the basics of breeding and training some of the best racehorses in the business. And for things with Sophie to be back to normal. But he bit his tongue and sucked in a breath over his coffee cup.

If everything on the farm wasn't in perfect shape, there would be hell to pay from Sophie, and there was nothing in this world he avoided more.

Distracted by the list in his head of things he needed to take care of before the end of the day, he hadn't been paying attention to the conversations around him. He was jolted back to the present by the ice-cold orange juice now soaking into his lap.

"Ugh!" Claude pushed his chair back.

"Max, say you're sorry to Claude for dumping your juice in his lap," Sergei scolded. He scooped up his son while Addison jumped up and began mopping up the table.

"Sorry," Maxim said. His cheeks were puffed out, and his eyes were downcast as Sergei moved Maxim to the edge of the room to wipe his sticky hands.

The seven-year-old was quite precocious and Claude had a soft spot for the boy. It tugged at his heartstrings in an unexpected way. The last time they'd visited, he'd spent quite a bit of time with the kids and the horses. Maxim was one of the reasons he'd finally, officially proposed. The time had come to listen to his gut, and to respect Sophie's biological clock's ticking, as she put it.

"Well, I think that's enough excitement for breakfast," Bertrand said, standing and pulling everyone's attention to him. "I actually gathered everyone here this morning for the unveiling of Claude and Sophie's wedding gift."

"What?" Sophie sputtered.

Bertrand clapped his hands. "Come, come. I have a grand surprise for you both." With that, he turned on his heel and stalked from the room. It was clear he expected everyone to follow. The scraping sounds of chairs against the hardwood filled the air as they all scrambled to catch up to him.

Claude assumed his soon-to-be father-in-law was going to show off his new attic office before showing everyone the new offices on the second floor. He didn't begrudge him this moment of attention. Bertrand had spared no expense on revamping the farm. It wasn't rundown, but the focus had always been on the horses, staff, and general maintenance, and not necessarily on updating the grounds themselves.

Marte stood against the counter, drying her hands on a towel in the kitchen as the entourage traipsed past her and up the back stairs. Claude grinned as she joined the line in the rear and followed him up. They bypassed the second floor, heading directly to the third-floor attic.

Maybe the engagement and upcoming wedding had put this in motion. Or Bertrand realized his little girl was all grown up and would be taking a far bigger role now. Or maybe retiring was on his mind. Claude didn't know for sure what the real reason was behind the mass changes, but since they were all for the betterment of the farm, he had no objection now the disruptions were mostly over.

He stepped into the vast open space and stopped, barely avoiding collision with Sergei and Maxim, who wrapped himself around his father's back like a sloth. A hush fell over them as Bertrand stood on the far side of the room, preening like a peacock, his arm around Sophie, who stood beside him. Her eyes were wide as she took in the place.

"Claude, come in and take a look," Bertrand said.

He patted Maxim's back and moved around them to see what it was that had Sophie's eyes bugging out of her head.

Confusion flooded in momentarily as he took in the changes to the room. He knew about the built-in bookcases, new dormer windows, refinished floors, and such. But what struck him speechless was the furniture in the room.

Not that the room was furnished entirely, per se. The shelves were empty, the walls bare, but in the middle of the room, centered directly between the two large dormer windows, two enormous, elaborately carved French oak executive desks sat facing each other. Stained glass lamps with heavy bronze bases perched at the edge of opposing corners. He had no doubt they were original Tiffany.

Only the lamp and a massive iMac monitor sat on each desk. There was little doubt, though, while minimal looking, the expense that had gone into it had been exorbitant.

He found himself at a loss for words as Bertrand and Sophie stared at him. It was finally dawning on him the purpose of the room. It wasn't a new office for Bertrand at all.

"Do you like it?" Bertrand asked.

"Papa, this is for us?"

"*Oui*. I thought a new domain suited you."

"I thought you were remodeling this space for yourself," Sophie said.

"*Oui*. It was to be a surprise. As the two of you will be partners in life, as well as in business, I thought it appropriate there be a special place the two of you could make your mark on."

"Bertrand, it's *magnifique*. Don't get me wrong, but I will be down in the stables most of the time, I won't need such a space," Claude said. He pulled his lip between his teeth. The sudden uncomfortable feeling in his stomach left him breathless.

"*Non*. You will be Sophie's equal here. Not only in the stables, but in making decisions on the best way for the farm to move forward."

Sophie nodded. "As it should be."

"I am the head veterinarian, nothing more." Claude's eyes narrowed at his fiancée and her father.

"Yesterday, maybe. Today, no more." Bertrand shook his head.

"I don't understand."

"The papers have been drawn up and signed.

You and Sophie shall be equal partners now. Both as veterinarians to the horses, and in all financial and business transactions for the stables as well."

Claude stood staring at Sophie, trying to gauge her reaction, but she seemed just as shocked as he was. The sparkle in her eyes relayed she was not upset, just surprised. He was torn. He knew the gesture was genuine, and he loved them for that. But at the same time, he was uncomfortable being the center of attention, especially when money was lavishly spent on him.

"Are you quitting?" Marte directed her question to Bertrand.

"*Non*, of course not. My office will be on the second floor, along with the new accountants and the other staff offices. But it will be Sophie and Claude running things once they return." He turned his attention to Sophie. "As you can see, the new computers arrived this morning."

"I thought you said no new hardware." Sophie directed narrowed eyes at her father.

Claude bit back a grin. He knew all too well what it was like being on the receiving end of those piercing eyes.

"Well, I couldn't very well have you deciding to meddle and ruin the surprise." An unrepentant grin split Bertrand's lips.

Sophie shook her head and laughed. It was infectious. Soon, everyone was clapping each other on the back and chatting while milling about.

"And your office, Papa?"

"It's not much different than this, just on a slightly smaller scale." He waved his hand around the room.

They began making their way down the stairs to see the second-floor renovations before heading out of the house to start their day. It was, as Bertrand described, a similar setup though on a much smaller scale.

Standing in the front of the house, Claude wrapped his arms around Sophie and kissed her before she climbed into the car with the women. They would be heading into the city for their final dress fittings, a spa day, and whatever else women did to prepare for big events. He didn't ask and really didn't want to know. The last time Sophie had tried to explain left him overwhelmed and exhausted.

He never wanted to endure that experience again.

Wedding Day

Sophie

S ophie sat stiff as a board, her hair and makeup expertly managed, and the dress so form-fitting she was certain eating dinner later would be a challenge. It was probably some cosmic twist of karma. Because she recalled teasing Addison about breathing being overrated when she'd complained about her own wedding dress being too tight.

The ladies gathered in the parlor of the house, sipping cucumber water and trying not to fidget while the professionals applied the finishing touches to their makeup or hair. Agnes and Marte had taken Addison's children and youngest sisters to the kitchen to bribe them with last-minute sweets before they were stuffed into their finery and not allowed to get dirty.

Glancing over at her friend, she couldn't believe they had known each other for the better part of a decade. Things had changed so much since she'd first met the shy American in Saint Petersburg, Russia.

Addison sat down beside her on the sofa.

"How are you holding up?" she asked.

"I'm feeling like a trussed-up Guinea keet at the moment."

"I can imagine. Can I get you anything?"

"More water would be appreciated," Sophie said. Afraid to move and mess up her dress, or something else, she handed Addison her glass.

"Just remember you are a trussed-up keet, going to the bathroom later will not be nearly as much fun as you think."

"Which is why I need to stay hydrated now." Sophie scrunched up her nose.

Addison took their glasses into the kitchen, leaving Sophie alone with her thoughts again.

"So, will you be waiting to have children, or will you be jumping right in like Addy did?"

It took a moment for Sophie to realize Tandy was sitting beside her.

"I'm sorry, what was that?"

"I was asking if you were planning on having children right away. God knows you could probably afford all the help you wanted if you haven't spent it all on this wedding."

"Mama!" Addison chided, coming back into the room.

Sophie's eyes were huge. There was a lump in her throat, preventing her from giving Addison's mother a much-deserved piece of her mind. Then again, it could have been the pleading look in Addison's eyes holding her tongue in check. Either way, she stared at Tandy, dumbstruck at her audacity. The woman was positively vulgar. Clearly, Addison had learned her manners from her father and stepmother.

"Mama, could you go check on the kids for me? Make sure Beth doesn't feed them too many treats?" Addison asked.

Tandy huffed. She stood and stalked out of the room to check on her youngest daughter and her grandkids.

Addison dropped into the spot Tandy had vacated and handed Sophie a glass. "I'm sorry."

"Can I please put a muzzle on her now?" Sophie whispered. Her hands gripped the dewy glass like a life preserver.

Tandy's snippy comments made the angst

lodged in her throat more challenging to ignore. Her morning had already started off terribly. The despair—trying to smother her—she'd woken up with was enough to make her reconsider getting out of bed all together. Another gut-wrenching dream had taken over, leaving her frazzled and restless. The thousand and one things that needed her attention or participation left her spent. She hadn't seen Claude in two days and the distance had tugged at her subconscious, leaving room for the cold, cruel visions to take further root.

Sophie needed to feel his arms around her, to see his face. It was the only thing that would soothe the emptiness.

There was no denying borrowing Addison's sisters for her bridal party had been a mistake since it had included inviting her mother along as well. Another reminder of the downside of being an only child. Having no large extended family on either side made it a bit more complicated to have the wedding of the century on your own.

Addison spat a mouthful of water out, spraying it down the skirt of her dress. "You're incorrigible." Her eyes grew wide at the wet spots all over her lap, and she fanned the fabric to dry it.

"I know. But I'm running out of patience with *that* woman."

"One more day, and then she'll be gone, and you won't have to deal with her again."

"Promise?" Sophie held her little finger in the air.

Addison laughed. Hooking her smallest finger with Sophie's, she said, "Pinky promise," and tugged like a pinky handshake.

Moments later, Sophie and Addison were in stitches, listening to the commotion taking place in the other room. Squeals of laughter came from the children as they were put into their formal wedding attire. Loud complaints were vocalized by Maxim.

The bargaining between the littles and the adults was most entertaining. The children were masterful negotiators, begging for more sweets. All the while, Marte and Agnes threatened no more desserts for the rest of the evening if they didn't settle down. It was good to hear the two house-keepers teaming up to keep things in order.

A flash caught Sophie's eye as one of the photographers made her rounds through the house, capturing the women getting ready and the children before they managed to wreak havoc on their clean clothes. A couple of the photographers ushered everyone into the parlor for the final photographs before the ceremony began. The last pictures were snapped, and then the photographers exited the house to head to their assigned spots.

Sophie stood as music filled the air. The dragonflies in her stomach began to riot. Since she was a child, she was sure they weren't regular butterflies since they felt like far bigger wings than the usual beating around her insides. The room spun out of focus, and sudden dizziness and nausea overcame her. She stumbled backward until the back of her knees hit the chair. She had to sit down. Putting her head between her legs, she took shallow breaths, willing herself not to be sick.

"Breathe, honey. You're going to be fine," Addison said.

She rubbed circles on Sophie's back to soothe her.

"Is everything okay?" Bertrand asked.

"She just needs a moment to catch her breath."

Addison continued to rub gentle circles as Sophie closed her eyes and focused on breathing.

"Here, drink this." Addison pressed a cold glass of water into her hand.

"*Non*, I'll only have to pee again," Sophie moaned.

Those left in the parlor tittered.

"A sip won't change anything, but it might calm your nerves."

"I think I'll need more than water for that," Sophie said.

This brought on more chitters as the bridal party and the rest of the stragglers left the house.

Addison handed her the glass and then helped her stand. She walked with Sophie and Bertrand as they made their way down to the back of the property where the ceremony would take place. Addison straightened out the bottom of the wedding dress and laid out the veil in a perfect display of crystals and lace behind Sophie.

As the music for the procession began, Addison kissed her cheek before taking her place behind the other bridesmaids.

Sophie gave up counting her steps once she reached one hundred and was beginning to regret the design as she realized the true length before she reached the center gazebo where they would say their vows. She could only hope her father wouldn't let her fall on her face as everyone watched. That was certainly not the grand entrance she'd envisioned.

Bertrand rested his hand over Sophie's own hand that was tucked into the crook of his elbow. He leaned over and whispered, "You are as pretty as a princess, *mon fille.*"

"*Merci*, Papa." Sophie choked back the tears that threatened to spill down her cheeks.

The music for the wedding march began. Her father tugged at her frozen body as the melody of "*Le Cygne*" by Camille Saint-Saëns filled the air. It might not have been a commonly chosen song for a wedding march, but it was dear to her. As a child, she had often sat on her mother's lap as she played. This was one of her mother's favorite pieces.

Eyes swimming, she barely appreciated the colorful fabric chair covers. With every few rows, the color faded to a lighter tone, like an Ombre in reverse as they worked their way toward the center of the space. The closest chairs started out in a deep copper, then slowly transitioned into lighter shades of gold, then rose gold, and finally pale champagne.

She followed the procession blindly as her father led her down the centralized path that bisected the four clover-like lobes of seating which surrounded the enormous wrought-iron and bronze gazebo. The bower itself was buried under thousands of flowers, nestled serenely in the center of the encircling chairs where Claude stood waiting with the priest. A smile tugged at her lips as the groups of forget-me-nots and the dandelions peeked out in little batches to make them stand out more.

It was funny how, after sixteen painstaking months of planning and preparation to make her wedding the social event of the season, the only thing holding her attention was Claude. The way his eyes seemed to drink her in as her father continued leading them down the long petal-strewn path. The way the sun faded behind him, streaking the sky with soft colors and highlighted his profile like he was an angel sent from heaven. His lips curved into the smile that always stole her breath. The vise grip in her chest loosened a little more as each step brought her closer to him.

Her hands grew clammy around the stems of her bouquet. The perfectly fitted dress felt like it was squeezing her lungs against her spine. Her ears rang, competing with the muted background music. The four-inch heels strained her ankles and pinched her toes. A panic attack, or worse, all-out fainting at the altar, was not an option. Under no condition could her wedding go down in the history books as the world's funniest wedding blooper. She gripped her father's arm tighter and focused on breathing through her nose.

One foot in front of the other… You've got this. Just a few more steps.

By some miracle, her father had her at the

center, placed her hand into Claude's and kissed her cheek.

The world stopped spinning.

People say some moments can freeze time, tilting the earth off its axis. She'd never believed it until this moment. They were in a bubble, just the two of them. Her hand in Claude's, his thumb caressing hers. His smile lighting up his face.

The priest's spiel sped by with barely any notice. It wasn't until Claude began speaking his vows that her muddled brain returned to her body.

"Sophie, you touched my soul when we were children, and I've never looked back. I have never had a moment's doubt you were the one I was meant for. You make me laugh and chase away my sorrows. Your smile brightens my world. You are there even in my darkest of days. I strive to be a better man each day to be worthy of you. Because of you, I've learned such deep, unconditional love." Claude finished his passionate declaration.

Her eyes were swimming again, and she wondered if she'd be able to say her vows.

"Claude, you make me a better person. Your love and patience ground me. With you next to me, there is no mountain I can't climb, no feat I can't master. For as far back as I can remember, you have always been at my side. I have never loved anyone as I love you. You have been my friend. My confidant. My ally. You know me at my deepest level. Down to my core. I choose you. Everyday. Always. Even when we are at odds, I know you will always be there for me when I need you."

The minister pronounced them husband and wife, and Claude kissed her soundly, grasping her hands to prevent her from collapsing as she leaned heavily into him.

Their return down the aisle was lively as everyone stood and cheered. Claude whispered dirty comments in her ear and had her laughing so hard she was doing her best not to choke on air and trip them as they walked.

CHAPTER 10

Reception

Sophie

Sophie's attention darted around the grounds. There were just so many people scattered everywhere. She heaved a huge sigh as everyone's eyes were diverted to the photographers, their constant snapping of pictures were murder. Groups, families, various high-profile guests, and of the children playing on the lawn across from the large white tents set up for the reception kept the cameras' busy.

Thank heavens, they had over a dozen photographers taking pictures simultaneously or they would never make it to their own reception.

Sophie slipped away from the family photos and paused at the fruit table to catch up with her matron of honor. Addison stood to the side, filling a glass with the fruit-infused water from the elaborately sculpted ice carafe. The dozen ice sculptures stationed around the reception were one of the many frills she had been fascinated with when planning the wedding. At least this one was not only beautiful but practical as well.

"How on earth can I be so hot while there is a pleasant breeze in the air," Sophie muttered.

Addison laughed and pressed the cold water into her hand. Taking another glass and filling it, she took a deep gulp before responding. "I'm overheated as well."

Sophie wiped the condensation from the glass and slid her damp hands up her arms.

"Did you notice your husband's uncle flirting with my mother-in-law?"

Addison giggled. "Oh, yes. I think Sergei might be over in the corner with a voodoo doll practicing some serious juju!"

"Oh, dear. You think he would be really upset?" Sophie craned her neck to see Sergei's expression.

"Actually, quite the opposite. He'd love to see his uncle settle down. Yuri's never shown even the slightest interest ever. Though he dotes on all of Sergei's family. So, I wouldn't put any attempt at matchmaking past Sergei."

"I hope Claude is as understanding."

Addison pointed to the other side of the room where a small group of people surrounded the groom. "I think he's already seen them and doesn't look too upset, in my opinion."

Claude caught her eye, nodded discreetly in the direction of his mother, and winked. A wide grin split his face.

"I'll take that as approval!" Addison said.

Sophie laughed. "I agree. Thank heavens. Leila deserves some happiness of her own." She sipped her water, letting it cool her as she took a moment to enjoy all that went into this day.

Addison laughed. "Well, if the matchmaking goes well, we'll actually officially become family."

"We already are." Sophie nudged her arm.

"Yes, you are the godmother to my children. And my very best friend. But if your husband's mother marries my husband's uncle, I do believe that makes us legally bound."

"It would certainly make the holidays more interesting!" Sophie's grin widened as she clinked her glass against Addison's.

Sophie glanced around the tent. The sparkling chandeliers, that dangled over each of the tables under the decorated tent, glinted and glittered against the stark white canvas. The sun had set, and the lights gave the party a romantic feel against the darkening sky.

While they were not blinking as Claude had suggested that night in the stables, she knew he had to be rolling his eyes over the light fixtures. At least he wouldn't complain since they were shaped as frothy dandelions. She'd gone out of her way to introduce another of their special flowers into the decorations.

She was proud of the little touches she'd incorporated into the decorations that mattered the most to Claude. The floral arrangements all held copious amounts of forget-me-nots, Claude's chosen *'forgive-me'* flower whenever he hurt her feelings. And there were sculptures and lights designed as dandelions, the flowers they'd wished upon together since they were children.

He hadn't asked for much, and since it had taken him until the eleventh hour to even venture an opinion, she'd been determined to make sure his desires were met.

They were called to dinner, and Sophie kissed Addison's cheek before joining Claude so they could be announced.

Once they were seated, a flurry of activity ensued. Wine and champagne glasses were filled, and dinner choices were confirmed.

Sophie slipped her shoes off under her chair. Even sitting, her feet needed a moment to relax. Out of the corner of her eye, she spotted Claude tugging at the top button of his shirt. Once it released, he adjusted his tie to cover it and let out an audible sigh.

When he caught her watching him, he gave a little shrug and grinned.

She smiled in return before sipping from her water glass.

Dinner whizzed by. She didn't eat most of what was put in front of her, only nibbled, it seemed, before one plate was replaced with another.

Once the endless toasts were over, the melody of their first dance began, and she slid her feet back into her shoes as Claude took her hand and helped her from her chair.

As Daniel Bedingfield crooned, Claude wrapped her in his arms and held her close.

"You look lovely, *ma chérie*. Good enough to eat," he whispered into her hair.

"How can you even think about food right now? Aren't you stuffed?"

"I'll always have room for you, darling."

Sophie giggled.

"It wasn't as bad as I expected," Claude conceded.

"That's the best you can do? Did you not see the chandeliers over the tables? Or the flowers?" She tapped on his lapel where a forget-me-not peeked from the pocket.

"*Non*," he said with slow deliberateness. "I only have eyes for you."

"Well, Mr. Durand, you best look around then. I put a lot of work into this to make you happy," Sophie muttered.

"Ah, Mrs. Durand." He kissed the tip of her nose. "That you did. And, as always, it's a masterpiece. You've put on a wonderful event. Your best yet, I'd say."

Sophie could feel the heat rise to her cheeks. His praise meant the world to her. It didn't matter what detail or reason when he spotted her efforts; it was everything she could ask for. He didn't often notice all that went into the social events the farm hosted unless it interfered with her time with him. Then, he just complained.

"Do you really think so?" she was fishing for more compliments and wasn't going to be coy about it.

"*Oui*. I have observed everything down to the last detail. Even all the silver dandelions poking out of flowers and dangling over the tables. Thank you for including them. Though they don't seem to be much good for wishing on." He winked at her.

Sophie let out the breath she'd been holding. She leaned up and kissed him under the chin. "All my wishes have already come true. Let someone else have them now."

"Why, Mrs. Durand, I do think that might be the noblest of gestures I've ever seen from you!"

Sophie ignored his barb. "I like it when you call me that."

"And I like the way it sounds." He squeezed her a little tighter as the song finished.

The father and daughter dance followed, with Sophie in her father's embrace as he regaled her with funny anecdotes from her childhood. Things her mother had sworn him to secrecy about. Like telling him Sophie would be Claude's wife someday.

"Really, Papa?"

"Oh, yes, you were nine. I do believe he had made his intentions clear long before that, but your mother knew as she watched you play that you were two pieces of the same puzzle. You complemented each other in ways even she didn't understand. But she was certain this day would come."

"I wish she was here. I miss her so." Tears pooled in Sophie's eyes.

"As do I. But I know she's watching over us, and

she's proud of you. I'm sure she's up there reveling, even now, at just another moment where she was right all along."

Sophie sniffed back tears. She didn't want smudged eyes in pictures of the happiest day of her life.

Bertrand hugged her close and kissed the top of her head. "No more tears now. Today we are celebrating only."

"Yes, Papa." Sophie dabbed at her eyes with her knuckles to avoid smearing her makeup as her father escorted her back to Claude.

To her delight, Sophie watched as Sergei's uncle Yuri led Leila onto the dancefloor. Off to the side, wrapped in Claude's arms, they watched another love match forming.

As the evening came to a close, she found herself wishing the night could last longer, while at the same time longing for a steaming bubble bath with some scented candles and Claude massaging her neck. Looking around again, she smiled. Everything had been perfect. So why was there a rock in the pit of her stomach?

CHAPTER 11

Frolicking with Elephants

Claude

C laude peered out of the dirty window of the rickety *angkot* they were in as it traveled down one of the worst roads he could remember being on. The roads in Bali were pocked and beaten. Streams of water carved their way across the path in many places, leaving them to bounce and shimmy as they made their way from the resort. Still, he was excited to be with Sophie. He had planned the entire honeymoon on his own, as a surprise. They had traveled to many places together, but never Indonesia, so he thought this would be a perfect place for them to start their adventures as a married couple.

Sophie clenched his hand every time the vehicle

lurched or swayed, and he would caress the top of hers with his thumb.

"Are you okay?" Claude asked.

"Yes, I just think the road is wreaking havoc with my breakfast. That's all." Sophie had a forced smile plastered to her face.

She exhaled in relief once the dreaded bus stopped.

"Here." Claude slipped a silk handkerchief into her hand, and she patted the moisture beaded along her brow.

The beauty that surrounded them was breathtaking as the group stepped out of the bus. It was a far cry from the scenery viewed from the window. The town they'd driven through looked worn out, but they were in the middle of an oasis. A tropical paradise if there ever was one.

He stood by as Sophie did a little pirouette in place, trying to take it all in. The rest of the group dispersed.

There were thousands of colorful flowers everywhere. Plumeria and orchids in pots and hibiscus thick in planters. Fragrant rainbow eucalyptus trees planted along the walkways and shrubs painstakingly carved into various shapes, including animals. Lotus flowers floated above the large koi in the numerous ponds, connected with small waterways that dotted the landscape.

Sophie pointed them out and told him what she liked about each, their colors, their aroma, their ability to withstand the heat, or the cold. It was a crash course in botany, but Claude loved seeing her so animated.

As they strolled through the botanical gardens, Sophie stopped and cupped a jasmine branch before bringing her face down to inhale deeply. As they headed toward the main building, designed to look like something out of an African safari, they noticed a small private wedding ceremony taking place.

Claude took her hand as they walked through the museum at the back of the great hall. An enormous mammoth skeleton held a prominent position in the center of the lobby. Tall, thick wooden beams crisscrossed the walls and ceiling. The walls, painted a muted beige, disappeared behind the many prints hanging on them.

The scenes were all safari in nature, with pachyderms the focus. One wall was covered in Asian elephants, the adjacent wall was full of the Sri Lankan elephant, and the far wall, at the end of the room, was filled with images of African elephants.

Some were frolicking in the water or passing through the desert in a line. And yet another of a mother and her baby near Mount Kerinci. The images depicted the stages of the Sumatran elephant's life cycle, including some that were clearly taken by amateur photographers in the field. The Gunung Leuser National Park was brought to life all around them as they crossed through the building.

There was a sudden, inexplicable longing deep within him to visit Africa. To drive alongside the Serengeti and watch the wild animals play along the plains. The discovery center, designed for children, was full of other unique artifacts that educated people about the life and habits of the pachyderms. This feeling of wanderlust was unusual for him. It was far more typical for Sophie to yearn for adventures far from home.

As they exited the building, an outdoor veranda and restaurant came into view on the left, facing a large man-made pond in the center of the courtyard. Four baby elephants played in the water and sprayed each other, using their trunks. The atmosphere was calm and serene. Palm trees danced in the slight breeze, easing the discomfort of the oppressive humidity in the air.

Holding hands, Sophie and Claude made their way to the stand to put their names in for an elephant ride. Moments later, a full-grown elephant was led over to them. The guide introduced them to Desi the elephant and then helped them up into the double seats strapped to her back.

"Thank you. Such a wonderful way to spend the day." Sophie set her head against his shoulder.

"I'm glad you're pleased. I wanted to see if the sanctuary lived up to its reputation. I think they've done a fabulous job creating a natural habitat for the elephants."

The elephant meandered slowly down the path and through the bamboo trees and foliage surrounding the sanctuary. They passed the back of the pond where calves played, and a pasture where the adult elephants were corralled to relax. Others were being bathed or playing with their young.

"How did you hear about them?" she asked.

"It was in one of the magazines you had lying around on destination weddings," he said.

"You looked through those?"

"Of course. I was surprised you were considering a wedding anywhere other than the farm, so I was curious."

"Oh, I wasn't. I was just looking at ideas for decorations, thinking outside the box, you know. So, you read about this place?"

"There was a brief article about animal sanctuaries and safaris, etc. and it got me to thinking about the honeymoon. I thought this would be different. I wanted more than to just sit on a beach for a couple of weeks."

A fragrant breeze danced through the flowers. Sophie snapped pictures of their surroundings as fast as she could.

"What made you zero in on this particular one?" she asked.

Claude waved his hand in the air. "This park is the only elephant sanctuary in Indonesia, and one of the largest of rescued Sumatran elephants. They have gone above and beyond, trying to implement the highest standards for the care of the animals and the conservation of the land around them."

"Ah, so you were thinking of the horses, weren't you?"

"*Oui*, I thought we could check this out and see if there was more we could do around the farm to make it greener and eco-friendlier."

Sophie laughed.

He was always butting heads with Bertrand about the changes to the farm. But after the initial brouhaha, his father-in law-seemed to slowly and quietly implement little steps in the direction he suggested.

"I think the farm needs more flowers and trees.

We have practical, and we have the small garden, but I'd like to see more color there," Sophie said.

"*Oui*, I think even your father would agree to the benefits as long as they are not poisonous to the animals."

A short time later, they were led back to the courtyard and helped down from their ride. Sophie snapped a picture of him standing next to the elephant and then handed the camera over to their guide to get one of them together.

The elephant was in a playful mood as she nuzzled her trunk against the side of his face. She wound her long nose around his shoulder. Like a jealous lover, she nudged and patted and maneuvered her bristly trunk in between them.

Sophie grinned at the animal's antics.

"Her adoration comes as no surprise. I just wouldn't tell Jezebel if I were you."

He chuckled.

Walking hand in hand with him, Sophie continued to steal glances over her shoulder back at what they termed to be their elephant. He had to tug her hand to keep her going in the right direction.

Once inside the restaurant, Sophie strode purposefully to the last table on the veranda at the edge facing the young pachyderms in their little lake. It was clear she couldn't get enough of them. He couldn't deny studying them from afar, while they were unaware they were being observed, was the perfect way to watch them.

The rest of the afternoon flew by in a blur. Claude had scheduled them a couple's spa treatment before they went for another walk through the botanical gardens, choosing a different paved trail than before. The heat was wearing Sophie out, so they headed back to the executive Taro suite they were staying in.

Stepping into the suite, Claude groaned at the immediate chill of the air-conditioned space and the ceiling fan circulating above. The machines had their work cut out for them, trying to beat back the heat from the open french doors. The contrast was remarkable.

After grabbing a bottle of water, Sophie made her way to the balcony and slipped off her sandals.

Standing at the doorway watching her, Claude said, "I'm going to wash up a bit before I join you."

Sophie nodded and plopped down on the chaise lounge, crossed her ankles, and took a deep swallow of the water.

He admired the grounds from between the slats of the banister.

When he came back out, she was fast asleep. He

called her name, but she didn't budge until he shook her shoulder.

"Hey, babe, let's take a nap. The bed looks pretty inviting." He gave her a mischievous grin.

"I'm sure it does, you fiend." She giggled.

He helped her stand, and she knocked over the open water bottle, splashing her feet.

"Ugh. I'm sorry. Did I get you?"

"Nah, go dry off and come to bed." Claude laughed.

CLAUDE WAS ALREADY SPREAD OUT AND SOFTLY snoring when she came in. A wooden mirror, carved with elephants, hung over the dresser. The partial coverlet at the foot of the bed had embroidered elephants strolling across in a line. Everywhere she looked, there were delicate reminders of the majestic animals.

After sliding onto the bed without disturbing her husband, Sophie curled onto her side and laid her head on his arm. *Her husband.* She hadn't really given much thought to those words until that moment. She was still the same person as a week ago and yet felt different somehow. More complete. It was just a piece of paper. Though their bond remained the same as it had been since childhood, something inside her changed. Lying there in his arms, contentment washed over her as she rested her eyes and enjoyed the moment.

HE WOKE HER AS THE SUN DAWNED OVER THE horizon with gentle kisses to her neck and by caressing her breast. With a moan, her body instinctively arched, pushing up against his hand. Her eyes popped open, and she pulled his head down to easily reach his lips.

Their tongues battled, darting in and out of each other's mouths. She nipped his bottom lip, and his sharp intake of breath made her bolder. Her kisses became more demanding as the blood rushed through his limbs.

He slipped his hand under her silk nightshirt and roamed. His fingers stroked her body, dancing along her ribs, gently pinching and circling her nipples, bringing them to life as they pebbled. Another moan escaped.

Sophie reached below the elastic waistband of his silk pants. He was already hard as she wrapped her hands around his shaft. His cock pulsated and throbbed as she skimmed her fingers from his base to the head.

The passion between them flared hot and explosive. Their lovemaking was quick and frenzied as if they had not coupled in too long.

Claude was exhausted. Sophie's screams had pulled him from a solid sleep, and it had taken a while for her to calm down. Her chest moved up and down in rhythm to her breaths, letting him know she had fallen back asleep. He propped himself up and admired her relaxed features. How her eyes twitched even in sleep as if she was watching something important. He struggled to fall back to sleep and ended up watching her for hours wondering what could have her so agitated as to upset her during their honeymoon.

After breakfast on the veranda, again seated overlooking the small lake, they joined a group that helped bathe the elephants, and had the opportunity to talk to them as their individual handlers stood by. Their skin was so prickly. Almost like his chin when he hadn't shaved in days.

Their weekend respite in the sanctuary had been too brief. He hated to leave it behind. They were happiest among animals.

Three hours later, their group left the park and the bus headed back to their resort. They would be leaving the following morning for their final destination, the Island of Penida, just a few miles off the coast of Bali. There, he'd rented a house for the next two weeks. He would have her all to himself. Every single naked inch of her, if he had anything to say about it.

CHAPTER 12

Paradise Island

Sophie

Sophie stood at the banister and watched as others disembarked. The twenty-minute ferry ride, crossing the Badung Strait from Bali to Penida Island, had been uneventful. Getting their luggage on board the boat, and then off and into the rental car had not been. Not in the least. It wasn't the first time her penchant for overpacking had gotten her a heavy sigh or a sidelong glance from those tasked with maneuvering her bags.

She chose to ignore the not-so-subtle attitude about her suitcases and just enjoyed the fresh air dancing over the water and ruffling her hair. She was who she was, and packing light wasn't one of her personality traits.

"We're going to have to put your cosmetic bag under your feet," Claude said. Walking past her, he set the large graphite monogrammed leather cube on the floor of the passenger side of the car. At least he had refrained from lecturing her, once again, on the overabundance of personal items. She couldn't be held responsible for what would have happened to him had he done so.

There was a deep-seated desire in her, longing for the days of the past when women packed dozens of steamer trunks full of clothes and linens and miscellaneous essentials, and no one batted an eye. An era when planning and preparation were considered an essential trait and not an unnecessary luxury or a burden. Now, people behaved as though actual luggage was a nuisance, and everyone should be able to survive any trip simply from a single carry-on piece. Frankly, she found this attitude utterly ridiculous.

Sophie was tired and sweaty, with a thoroughly unladylike disposition. "That's fine." With a nod, she bit her lip and slid into the car, propping her feet on her toiletries. Claude shut her door and finished stuffing the luggage wherever it would fit. She would need another shower by the time they made it to the rental house.

The property Claude had reserved for their stay

sat isolated at the top of a small hill overlooking the city. Their little SUV rental chugged up the long, narrow, winding road. Sophie leaned her head out the window, taking in the majestic views of the strait and the Balinese mainland. The breeze carried sweet and floral scents into the car, easing some of the tension in her shoulders.

Claude helped her from the car, leaving the luggage behind. After swooping her up into his arms, he carried her into the house and set her down in the open living area.

"It's beautiful." Sophie twirled around, kicking off her sandals.

The house held the same Indonesian-themed charm as the villa they'd stayed in, and the suite at the elephant sanctuary. The sand travertine floors were cold under her bare feet as she stretched her toes against the smooth squares. The two walls facing the back of the property held large, accordion-style, panoramic, floor-to-ceiling glass doors.

The glass partitions disappeared against the sidewalls, making the room airy and comfortable with an unobstructed view of the world below. This gave one the feeling of being outside while within. The remaining walls were paneled in dark wood.

With renewed exuberance, she tugged at Claude's hand, pulling him out to the terrace.

"Come," she said. With his hand in hers, she rushed them to the balcony. Leaning over the polished, gleaming dark wood banister, they took in the view together.

There wasn't another house to be seen. They had the entire mountaintop to themselves. The waves crashing against the cliffs below and the birds chirping as they rested in the surrounding trees were the only sounds invading their solitude.

"Do you like it?" Claude asked.

"It's perfect." Sophie turned and wrapped her arms around his neck. "I love this place," she said before leaning against him and kissing his waiting lips. His arms tightened around her, bringing her closer as he deepened the kiss. When he pulled away, she was breathless. Even after all the years together, he still made her knees weak and her heart to skip a beat.

"I need to wash up. I feel sticky," she said.

"Want me to wash your back?" The mischievous glint in his eye betrayed his thoughts.

"Sure, need help with the luggage?"

"No, I've got this. I'll meet you there."

With a giggle, she headed across the open floor plan to the back of the house, to where she assumed was the probable location of the master suite.

Each door and window splayed out, letting

more of the outside in. There were delights to be seen through each of the exterior doorways she passed. The first showed a koi pond. Long, rectangular stone steps crossed through the center and a life-sized Buddha statue overlooked it. A second doorway led to a small courtyard with a shaded gazebo in a garden. Bamboo trees, in large, ornate, alabaster pots, also lined up against the back wall, sat centered at each window she passed. It was like having living artwork framed in each pane of glass.

The master bedroom was simple. A bed, a dresser, and what looked to be a long, enclosed closet at the far side. As she passed each piece of furniture her fingers lingered on their smooth surface. It was as though she wanted to absorb its beauty to remember forever. Another wall of sliding glass doors opened onto the back terrace and a waterfall. The bathroom was enormous. A long teak vanity rested against one wall. An oversized, basin sink of chiseled stone sat centered on a granite countertop, stone Frangipani flowers adorning each side of the mirror.

At the end of the long rectangular room, a shower filled the corner. There was no glass door to enclose it. It was long, deep, and spacious. The area more resembled a tiled carwash than a regular shower stall. The two large, square showerheads in the high ceiling could probably drown a person if they weren't careful. Floor-to-ceiling tiles covered the only two walls of the stall and then opened entirely at the end, where it was exposed to the outdoors.

The lingering sounds of the fountains flowing, and the birds chirping echoed around her.

Hmm. No bathtub. That's disappointing. Curious to see the view, Sophie advanced into the shower space. It was breathtaking. An enclosed garden full of bright exotic flowers and plants greeted her as she walked through the exposed shower stall. Situated in a stepped pedestal was a large soaking tub cut into the ground that would hold two comfortably. It reminded her more of a rectangular Jacuzzi than a bathtub. A bamboo ladder leaned against the outside wall, fresh towels folded over its rungs.

Now we're talking.

A bronze faucet, fashioned like a cut bamboo shoot protruded from the back wall. The water flowed like a waterfall into the tub. Sitting on a tray to the side were glass containers of scented bath beads and foaming bath gels. After she liberally poured both into the streaming water, the aroma of orange blossoms and lemongrass billowed forth.

Setting a loofa on the tub's edge, next to a

plastic bottle of body wash, she shut the water off and ran her hand under the bubbles to check the temperature, satisfied.

Peeling sweat-soaked clothes from her body, she let them slip to her feet and stepped down into the tub. Clouds of foaming bubbles floated around her as she lowered her body into the lukewarm water. It was pure heaven.

Claude fumbled with the luggage in the bedroom, if the muffled curses and thumps of the suitcases hitting the ground were any indication. This brought a smile to her face, and she forced herself not to laugh. She had offered to help, only to be told it wasn't needed. The least she could do is not rub proverbial salt in his wounds.

"Ah, there you are. A bath? Splendid." Claude scrambled to undress, dropping his clothes where he stood and climbed the steps to the bathtub.

What a magnificent body. Her breath stuck in her throat. She never tired of watching him as his muscles flexed when doing the smallest of tasks. He was in excellent shape from the years of working with horses. Sometimes, she felt the need to pinch herself. Remind herself it—he—was real.

As he slipped under the water, she slid back to make more room for his legs. They sat facing each other, listening to the birds chirp on the other side of the wall, letting the water wash away the sweat and sea air from their skin.

"Scoot over here, I promised to wash your back."

"*Oui*, that you did." Sophie twisted around, sloshing water to and fro, as she slid across the bench into his waiting arms.

As Claude picked up the loofa and gently rubbed circles on her skin, she could feel his excitement grow. She pushed herself tighter against him and smiled when his hand paused on her shoulder. After a moment, the loofa moved again as his hard sex throbbed against the small of her back.

Trying to relax under the water, letting his massage clear her mind as well as her sweaty body, she found herself distracted by his growing desire. To test his interest, she wiggled her butt a little, rubbing against him. She bit her lip as the circles paused again, and he groaned. He leaned in and nipped at her earlobe, her chest constricting as he grated his teeth gently across the lobe.

She deliberately glided against his hardness again, back and forth. The sound of his heavy breathing told her he was just as distracted.

With a splat, the soggy loofa landed on the stones outside the tub, and Claude's hands found their way to her hips. Gripping her gently, he lifted her to his lap. He slid her hair over her shoulder and kissed the back of her neck. His cock pulsated against her ass as his lips grazed her skin, causing goosebumps to rise on her arms and chest. Her body trembled. As she moved to turn, his hands tightened their hold on her hips, keeping her in place.

"Fold your legs under," he whispered in her ear. He lifted her up again, and the water sloshed as she did as he instructed. As he lowered her back against him, he maneuvered her perfectly over his extended cock and slid into her.

He was deep inside her as she moved slightly forward, the friction causing her body to vibrate. His breath came out in a hiss, letting her know the same sensations coursed through him. The fingers on her hips dug into her flesh.

Biting her lip, she pressed back, sliding him deeper still and resting against his stomach. His breath hitched as he nestled his lips behind her earlobe and kissed the side of her neck. Her heart thudded as blood raced through her body. She wiggled her ass, just enough to increase the fluttering feeling.

Sophie repeated this as her muscles tightened, and the intensity of the orgasm increased. Tingles started in her toes and through her legs. Her muscles flexed involuntarily, and the twitching ebbed and flowed as her momentum sped up. The pulsing of blood pounded where they connected.

Claude gripped her hips even tighter, though not taking control of her movements, but letting her set the pace.

As her orgasm consumed her, her head spun. Claude's followed moments later, his breathing coming in heavy pants as his face pressed against her shoulder and her chin tucked against her chest.

CHAPTER 13

Making Waves

Sophie

Sophie stepped out of the clear, blue, crescent-shaped pool and shook out her hair. Water dripped from her body as she made her way back to the chaise lounge. The patio overlooked the edge of a cliff, giving her a view of a valley of trees below. The infinity-edge on the far side of the pool gave the illusion of the water cascading down into the ocean below.

There was this inexplicably strong feeling she had been in this very spot before, but she had never actually been here. Followed by a sense of foreboding. It had to be because she was exhausted and needed some down time.

Propping herself against the oversized pillows,

Sophie perused her endless pile of to-be-read books sitting on the table beside her, waiting for Claude to return from his day hike. While Claude was a ball of energy, she was exhausted. They had returned early that morning from their overnight stay in the Nusa Penida Treehouse at the Thousand Island Viewpoint, and she longed for a day of rest.

The treehouse was undoubtedly one of the best attractions on the island so far. A spectacular spot overlooking the coast and the pounding of the surf against Atuh Beach. The stairs up and down and the constant walking and swimming had worn her out. Crossing her ankles, she considered their stay so far. It was hard to believe they had been on Penida Island for more than a week. The days were blurring.

Their adventures began on the third day on the island. First, they had visited the Pura Goa Giri Putri Cave. Climbing the narrow and winding staircase to reach the cave halfway up the mountain had been rough.

The next day had been filled with snorkeling with the giant manta rays in Manta Bay, followed by a trek to the Peguyangan Waterfall the day after. Sophie had been momentarily convinced the steep blue stairs would be the death of her. Only the promise of spectacular views of the cliffs and coast below made her press on. Reaching the sacred temple and waterfall, as well as witnessing a local participating in a water blessing, made the effort worth it.

Then the night at the treehouse—though she loved everything they had done—her body was rebelling. Worn out, she wanted nothing more than to sit by the pool, soak up some rays, and catch up on her reading.

At breakfast, Claude had suggested a day of sunning by the pool, giving her a reprieve from the exertion of their adventures and all of those endless stairs. He went on a hike with Markus and Sven, a couple of the guys they had met while staying at the small villa on Bali. They were on the island for the day and would be returning via the ferry before dinner. She just didn't have the energy for any more excursions, and since the men had come without their wives, the day's plans suited her perfectly.

She often thought of the elephants, though. The island had been relaxing but lonely, in a sense, at the same time. When Claude returned from his afternoon out, she hoped to talk him into a day trip back to Bali to revisit the sanctuary. It had been the highlight of their honeymoon by far.

The bright orb in the sky glinted brilliantly against the pool's water and warmed her skin. Restless, she stretched her legs on the lounge chair. Her mimosa sat on the table beside her, barely touched. She hadn't slept well. Even in a beautiful location, the nightmare had come again. This recurring dream of Claude leaving her had started in the months before the wedding, and she'd chalked it up to wedding jitters. Now, she wasn't so sure. Something was bothering her, and she couldn't put her finger on it even though things were great. Everything had fallen into place, exactly as she'd always dreamed. Her life was perfect.

The days seemed to merge in blissful nothingness as she lounged by the pool or in the hot tub each evening with Claude. Relaxing with a glass of wine under the setting sun, with its vivid array of colors crossing the sky each night, it was nothing short of spectacular. Being higher than the city lights gave them an unfettered view of the night sky and the splashes of color above them. The entire stay had been nothing short of a scene out of a bestselling romance novel.

Except for the damn nightmares, life was perfect. And those needed to find someone else to torment because she was the happiest she'd ever been.

A LOUD SMACK JOLTED HER AWAKE. AS SHE SAT upright, her head swam, and she blinked rapidly while the bright sun blinded her. It took a moment to get her bearings. She'd fallen asleep by the pool. When the nightmare had hit her with the force of a dozen bricks, it had scared her enough to flinch and send her phone careening to the ground. The sound of the metal against tile pulled her from its ugly grip. This one had been nastier than usual—darker and colder, somehow. She was being smothered by some invisible hand crushing her face. It wasn't the usual endless reaching in vain for Claude. She glanced over at the half-full mimosa glass and melted cheese on the plate beside it. Her stomach growled in response.

Her book smashed to her chest. With a groan, she leaned down grabbed her phone and sighed at the time. No wonder she was starving. Lunch had passed her by. Her breakfast had been light, and her body had metabolized that hours ago. After pressing the bookmark in the center of the page, she closed the book and put it on the table. She strolled through the spacious entertaining area and into the kitchen to find sustenance. Claude hadn't given her a definitive answer on when he expected to return. So he'd not likely be home before the last ferry left the island for Bali around sunset. Sophie reached for her phone to see if he'd called or texted. Fingers on the buttons, she considered sending him a text to tell him she missed him but then paused. He was with friends and she didn't want to be *that wife* always nagging him to spend time with her.

She needed to fill her grumbling stomach. After pulling things out of the refrigerator, she set up an array of snacks on the counter. She took the carafe from the bottom shelf, and, as her fingers touched the condensation, the glass pitcher slipped a little, sloshing the liquid over the edge. *Damn it.* She sighed, looking down at the small pool of tea on the tile.

Stretching to place the carafe on the counter, there was a sharp tremor under her foot, and she stepped into the puddle. *Merde.* Another vibration, harder than the first, made the tea only slosh a bigger mess around her. The carafe slid out of her hand and shattered as it struck the tile below. The floor rolled as she grasped for the edge of the counter, the glass shards ignored, as she struggled to remain standing.

Glass crunched as her bare foot landed in the center of the mess. Slicing into her skin like minuscule razor blades, the pain radiated up her leg and instinctively, she jerked it back up. A third shudder in the ground took her balance finally, and her legs flew out from under her. Her mind seemed to have no control of her limbs. She was falling. The lurching in her stomach told her so. Her hands flailed as she clamored for anything to stay upright. Nothing slowed her descent. It felt like everything was happening in slow motion as the room flashed before her eyes. Sophie's last coherent thought, as she was sliding toward the ground, was of Claude when her head struck the edge of the counter and blackness overcame her.

CHAPTER 14

Male Bonding

Claude

C laude sat with his hands in his lap as his friends paddled their kayaks closer. Their day had begun with a strenuous hike at sunrise until Sven twisted his ankle. So, after a quick lunch, they had settled into an afternoon on the water. It hadn't been expected.

Sitting on the water and letting the animals come to him was far more relaxing than snorkeling or scuba diving. The air was thick and humid. It felt like drinking water into his lungs. A wide grin developed at the men's laughter as they raced each other to meet him in the center of the inlet. He had beaten them by a long shot, though, he knew Markus had put little effort into it. Had

Markus even tried, he'd have left them miles behind in his wake. The afternoon was peaceful with their small group, the only ones left out in the water. The shore was dotted with people who lounged on large blankets or oversize beach towels.

The small island was full of wonders. Every moment they'd spent on it had been an experience to remember. He could feel himself growing hard at the thought of Sophie waiting at the house for him, wearing nothing but the skimpy bikini she'd had on at breakfast. He'd seen more fabric in a napkin. Knowing she planned to sun herself at their pool alone, he had no reason to object—he was the only one to see her in it, so he grinned suggestively.

Sophie would love the way the fish and other sea animals bobbed their heads up around their little plastic boats to observe them before sliding back under the waves. He would have to bring her out there before they left the island. It was a completely different experience than snorkeling or scuba diving. A sense of peace came from sitting in the middle of the small inlet as the water lapped against the kayak's sides, gently rocking him back and forth while he watched the beach.

Small children danced at the edge of the shore, dipping their toes in the foamy waves before giggling their way back to the sand and over to their waiting mothers.

Claude inhaled the salty air deep into his lungs and enjoyed the moment. He watched a frisbee game, a couple of children chasing a dog at the edge of the surf, and a young couple building an elaborate sandcastle, just far enough away from the water to be safe from the incoming waves.

Over the years, he'd often spent hours with Sophie at one of the little sidewalk cafés, enjoying a bottle of wine and people watching. They would pick out people going about their business and guess what their plans or destination could be. Like lying in the meadow and pointing out puffy animal-shaped clouds in the sky when they were children, it was one of their favorite pastimes. Sophie's imagination was so over the top they would end up in hysterical laughter at the story she painted for the strangers they saw.

Sophie's image swam into his thoughts. Missing his wife, his interest in the adventure with the boys waned, and he decided to head back to their little rented slice of paradise. A nice romantic dinner in the small town at the bottom of their hill was in order.

No sooner had these plans crossed his mind, there seemed to be commotion on the shore. He heard loud voices in the distance. They were raised just enough to carry sound, but not the actual words. Instead, there was only confusion at what he saw but didn't quite understand.

Children were trudging through the soft sand to their frantic parents as fast as their short, pudgy legs could carry them, the dog close on their heels. The adults waved their arms in the air and continued to call out, but Claude wasn't sure of the purpose. He assumed it was to pull the children from the water, but glancing around him, he saw no sign of a shark or any other animal activity.

The waves beat against the hull of his small craft, but they weren't oversize. He didn't see any logical reason for the change in atmosphere, though it wouldn't be the first time he'd been accused of being obtuse.

Sven sat in his kayak, a few feet away. He motioned his hand, signaling they should head back to shore. Markus was already ahead of them by a good stretch, looking over his shoulder in alarm, clearly concerned about the excitement on the beach. He, too, pointed toward the shore to return to land.

Claude grabbed his oar and paddled against the heavy waves. It was as if he was spooning molasses. His thrusts against the water were strong, but he wasn't making any headway. The shore appeared just as far away as it had before he'd put the oar back in the water.

He continued pulling himself forward. The water, however, seemed hellbent on pushing him farther out of the inlet instead of toward the shore.

His kayak bounced around the water like he had entered a typhoon, but a quick glance at the sky showed no change. The blue sky was punctuated by the occasional white puffy cloud, so the threat wasn't from above. The water churned all around him as he tried to match Sven's pace. Markus had pulled even farther ahead, though, not a huge surprise considering his history as an Oxford rower.

The inlet was no longer stable. He glimpsed Markus up ahead, just a dot against the churning water. Sven called out to him, and Claude turned his head toward his voice, but Sven's kayak was upside down, bouncing along the waves like a top.

Claude called his name over and over, but Sven's head never surfaced. Fear gripped his gut as he shoved his oar in the water, and, in punishing strokes, tried to reach his friend. His last sight was Sven's bright orange plastic craft bobbing up and down unoccupied.

A wave he hadn't expected slammed into him

and threw him from his boat. He let out a strangled scream as his head slipped underwater and back up again.

His voice cracked as he swallowed the water pounding against his face. He knew he must be close to where Sven was last, but he couldn't see him. Claude's boat hit the side of his head in a brutal blow. The pain was excruciating as the water continued its assault, pulling him below, only to shove him back up again. He couldn't get his bearings.

Memories of Sophie's beautiful face, smiling as she danced with him at their wedding just a few short weeks ago, filled his mind. He would never see her again. The thought crushed him as he choked on another wave, trying to tread the water so determined to drown him.

Another wave smothered him, and then there was no pain, no gasping for air, or grasping for the line that tied him to his boat. *Nothing.*

CHAPTER 15

A Whole New World

Sophie

"Hello? Ms. Sophie? Mr. Claude?"

A voice calling her name drifted through the fog surrounding Sophie's mind.

Pain radiated through her body. It wasn't Claude's voice, though it was male. His slight accent said he was a local, though her eyes were full of grit, and she couldn't see clearly.

As she tried to push herself up, sharp stabbing pains shot through her flat palms and arms and she cried out. Blood pooled in them as she stared at her injured hands.

The man called her name again. Glancing up,

she saw him standing at the edge of the island, peering down at her.

She didn't recognize the man, though something told her she should. Her head hurt, her hands throbbed, and her eyes felt like they'd been washed in sandpaper.

"Ma'am, don't move. There is glass everywhere. Let me sweep some up before you injure yourself further."

Sophie just nodded. She wasn't sure what was going on, or why she was on the floor in a puddle of blood and glass.

There was a vague memory of another dark dream, waking by the pool, preparing lunch, and then there had been tremors. She didn't recall what happened after that, the more she tried to fill in the gaps in her memory, the more her head hurt.

"Okay, ma'am, I'm going to sweep up the areas around you first. Then I'll take this damp cloth and see about getting the glass off you. Your hands are the only thing bleeding at the moment, but there is blood all around you, so I'm sure you have more cuts."

He went about gently moving the shards away from her as he calmly explained he was the caretaker of the property. "I apologize for the delay in coming up the hill to check on things."

"It wasn't long, really. I'm assuming it was an earthquake," Sophie said.

"Yes, ma'am. A couple of earthquakes, in fact. And then the tsunami came right after."

"A tsunami? Did it do much damage?"

"Yes, ma'am. The main roads have been closed for the last day, and many others are still."

"The last day?"

"Yes, ma'am. The earthquake hit after eleven AM yesterday morning. It's three o'clock in the afternoon now on Thursday."

"It's been a whole day?"

"Yes, ma'am. I'm sorry. I tried to call, but the lines are not working yet, and the only road up the hill was blocked by a downed power line."

"I see." She really didn't, though. Her eyes were still cloudy, and she certainly didn't understand anything. It was like her brain was still stuck on the floor with all the glass.

"There we go, let's get you up, now." He helped her to her feet, away from the pile of glass that had once surrounded her. Sophie winced as he held her arm, and they walked over to the couch. He set a thick throw down on the cushions. His face turned away, not meeting her eyes. It was like he was embarrassed.

In her confused state, it took her a minute to realize she was still wearing her barely-there bikini.

"I'm sorry, I don't recall your name," she said.

"Niko, ma'am."

"Niko, would you mind grabbing my swimsuit cover-up from the lounger by the window? I'm sorry, I wasn't expecting company when I put my suit on to sunbathe."

"I understand, ma'am. I'll be just a minute."

As though the building was on fire, he fled from the open lounge area and returned a moment later, holding her knee-length coverup. An arm shoved it at her as he stood off to her side, still not looking directly at her.

The tension visibly left his shoulders as she slipped the soft cotton wrap on and tied the belt around her waist.

"I can try to have Esmeralda come up, in a day or two, to clean for you—but I haven't been able to reach her, either."

"I understand. That isn't important right now."

Niko nodded in understanding.

"I'm confused. You said I've been on the floor—unconscious, apparently—for over a day? And where is Claude?"

"I'm sorry, ma'am. I have not seen your husband. I came as soon as I could."

Sophie stared at him; she could barely process the idea of being out cold, on a floor, for over a day. The hollowness in her gut reminded her of the nightmares she'd been experiencing for the better part of the last year. An emptiness as she reached for Claude and never felt his touch. The terror within, he was gone forever.

"We should probably get you down to the clinic. They can treat your wounds, so you don't get an infection, and check your head since you were knocked out for so long."

His comments pulled her from her meandering thoughts.

"I need to stay here in case Claude returns."

"You can leave him a note to let him know where you are. And he might already be at the clinic looking for you, ma'am, since he wouldn't have been able to get up the hill before I did."

"Okay. I need to put some real clothes on. I can't go into town dressed as I am."

"Yes, ma'am. That would be a good idea." Niko nodded with more enthusiasm than she thought possible for the small man.

Sophie hobbled to the master bedroom and took stock of what she had. Her hands fumbled as she gingerly peeled her cover-up off, let it tumble to the floor, and untied the bikini strings, making the pieces fall as well. She was grateful the bra had a front clasp, or she'd have never managed it by herself. A sundress seemed the best option for now —she would be fully covered, but able to move around.

Niko helped her into his little rickety pickup truck having seen its best days more than a decade before. But it didn't matter much to her, she was grateful for his assistance. He made small talk during the drive, telling her stories of what he'd seen on his way up the hill.

Sophie was distracted as her thoughts were only of Claude. Where he was, if he was injured and in need of help. A distinct sense of aloneness crept in.

When they arrived at the clinic, chaos reigned. It was a madhouse like nothing she'd ever seen before. The noise made her head throb harder. Her eyes watered at the strain to take it all in.

There were crying adults and inconsolable children. Animals ran amok in the makeshift triage area, in what probably served as the parking lot. The noise was excruciating. The pounding of her headache only increased, surrounded by all the commotion.

The doctors who were busy treating the more

serious injuries waved her off after an initial glance at her much less severe cuts and scrapes.

After a quick walkthrough to see if she could locate her husband, she realized how understaffed and overwhelmed they all were. Making her way back to the front, she found a nurse dealing with the scrapes and cuts of a handful of wayward children.

"Ma'am, I'd like to offer my assistance if I could," Sophie said.

All thoughts of her own injuries and her missing husband vanished as her training flooded her mind. The doctor in her kicked in instinctively as it was clear more help was needed.

"What can you do?" the nurse asked, not looking up from wrapping a sling around her young patient.

"Back home in Paris, I am a veterinarian."

"Ah, an animal doctor. This is good." She patted the young boy on the back and sent him on his way with a few words in the native language Sophie didn't understand. "Let's get you cleaned up first, so we don't contaminate the area and make everyone sicker."

"Good idea."

Sophie sat on the chair indicated, and the nurse made quick work of her hands and leg. Her foot wasn't as bad as she feared. It would hurt for a while, but the wound wasn't as deep as she'd expected for the amount of pain it produced.

The cut on the back of her shoulder required sutures but was cleaned up and managed quickly.

"You might have a concussion, but I think the danger has passed. You will have to take it slow and make sure you don't overdo it."

Sophie nodded then got to work. She helped with more minor injuries first. Once they'd managed that, they corralled the able children and asked them to safely round up any animals that looked injured. If the animals were agitated in any way or severely hurt, they were to leave them alone and return for an adult to assist them.

The children nodded before rushing out to fulfill their new duties.

Grinning, the nurse patted Sophie on the shoulder. "Thank you. That will keep them out of mischief and solve the problem of the animals at the same time. Brilliant."

Sophie returned her smile. It was the least she could do, caring for them while the nurses helped the doctors. Time passed, and the sun had moved toward the horizon. Sophie was exhausted. Most of the animals and children that had already been there when she arrived had been cared for, but more and more people streamed in each hour.

She had not found Claude, and while she asked everyone she could, no one recalled seeing him either. The phone lines were still down, including the cell towers. Generators had the electricity functional, for the most part. The only answer she could think of, regarding Claude, was that they had missed each other when she came down to the clinic. She was sure he must be back at their rental house, waiting for her.

The caretaker returned and offered her a lift home. He had a bag of fresh fruit and bottled water for her, and a plate of food his wife had made. After she settled into the small truck, he placed the food in her lap. It smelled divine. The spicy aroma assaulted her empty stomach, and it grumbled in protest.

This was a stark reminder she hadn't eaten since breakfast with Claude almost two days before. There was still no sign of her husband, but with all the confusion, she could only pray they were passing each other without knowing. The alternative always gut-punched her when she allowed herself to travel down that path of thought, so she made a point to push those thoughts aside though the experience left her shaken and disturbed.

After the long day spent at the clinic, she was drained—both physically and emotionally—and wanted nothing more than to crawl into bed with hopes that the morning would bring better news, and her husband home with her where he belonged.

CHAPTER 16

Bad Tidings

Sophie

S ophie sat on the veranda, staring out into space. The beautiful view went unappreciated as it barely registered through her fugue state.

She couldn't stop the dread that invaded as each day passed without any sign of Claude. The horrible dreams invaded her sleep every night, leaving her drained and battered. She worked at the clinic from sunup to sunset every single day, hoping the bone-deep exhaustion would leave her mind empty and allow her to rest even though she knew it was futile. It had been almost four weeks since everything upended, and life on the island had been slow to return to normal. The authorities promised to keep her informed if they learned anything. Still, she didn't have much hope left considering the number of missing people they were searching for.

Her father would be arriving at some point that day. It had taken a full week after the earthquake and tsunami before phone service had been stable enough to allow her to get a call through to Paris. Bertrand had been wearing the carpet thin, according to the reports from Agnes. In fact, it took Agnes a solid ten minutes to chronicle every detail of his state the previous week before she handed the phone to Sophie's father.

If the situation hadn't been so dire, Sophie would have found Agnes's histrionics comical. But she couldn't laugh. Claude was still missing, and their family had been unable to reach them on the island.

By the time Bertrand had taken over the phone, Sophie was more worse for wear, concerned about her family's well-being as much as her own.

It had taken every effort to convince her father to not hop on the plane the moment he heard her voice. He had only agreed to wait a few more days before flying over. If Claude hadn't appeared by the end of the week, there was nothing that would prevent him from coming.

She had been so certain of Claude's return that

she readily agreed. Though, it had taken her father longer to make the trip than he expected. When her father called the previous night to say he would be arriving in the afternoon, the air had fled her lungs in a rush. Since Claude had gone missing, each day had required her to put one foot in front of the other while her mind remained in a fog.

Niko drove up the hill each morning, bringing with him a cup of fresh coffee and a small breakfast burrito his wife made.

He dropped her off at the clinic on his way to join the able-bodied who continued to account for everyone. There were small groups going from house to house to provide bottled water until the water supply could be restored. Larger groups assisted humanitarian aid workers to clear the power lines and repair the sanitation system. Fire-fighters continued to battle small blazes that dotted the island. Others did search and rescue—and while she waited to be reunited with her husband, she tended the minor injuries of the animals and children.

Each day, she worked with the nursing staff, avoiding the doctors who treated her as though she was a nuisance because she was a woman and "*only* an animal doctor" as one of them had said. He treated everyone with the same disdain so, she made every effort to stay out of his way to avoid his barbed tongue lashing out at her.

It was of little consequence since the nurses were grateful for her presence. The days were long and demanding. They required so much of her uninterrupted attention, it wasn't until she returned to the house the reality of her missing husband slammed back into her.

All at once, the bliss of denial, the momentary peace of forgetfulness, vanished. Everything came back as a slap in the face, the moment she stepped back into the house and he was not there.

"Claude. Honey, are you home?" she called out each afternoon. It was a reflex. While her mind knew he was not and would not be there, her heart longed for his return so much she found herself shouting out to him each day. Only to have the sensation of a fist in her stomach at the suppressive silence greeting her instead.

Niko had taken the rental car to town to meet the ferry carrying her father. Niko seemed to love driving the newer car. Since it came with air conditioning—unlike his old pickup truck—she had no reservations about him driving her around in it. She was not in any condition to drive, still distracted by her turbulent emotions.

While sipping iced tea, Sophie was surprised by

the sound of a car approaching. It was way too soon for Niko to have returned from the docks.

A soft rap on the open door and a voice called out, making her heart stop.

"Hello?"

She raced to the front door, expecting to find her husband there. Her breath caught in her throat as their friend Markus stood on the threshold. Alone.

"Sophie. Ah, it's so good to see you. You are well?" he asked.

"I'm alive, but where is Claude? Is he not with you?"

"I'm so sorry, Sophie…"

Her head started spinning, and her knees buckled.

He lunged in time to catch her before she collapsed, leading her back to the veranda and setting her in the oversize chair she had been sitting in before he arrived.

He took the chair across from hers.

After a moment of silence, Sophie focused on her guest to avoid the battling emotions within. "I'm sorry. Where are my manners? Markus, would you like something to drink?"

"I'll get it, is the tea you're drinking in the icebox?"

"Yes, could you bring some extra glasses? My father should be here any minute."

"Oh, that is good," he said.

Markus made haste back to the kitchen, and she heard him opening and closing the cupboards. Sophie should have gone in and helped him to make it easier, but her legs were lead weights. Her gut roiled, warning her more bad news was coming. If Claude wasn't with him, and neither was Sven, then something was amiss.

I don't think I can take much more.

As Markus sat back down, a tray of glasses and a glass carafe of tea on the small table between them, another car pulled up. Car doors slammed; familiar voices filled the air.

Her already tight insides clenched further. The sudden urge to flee exploded within her as her mind scrambled to accept her father had not come alone. It was absurd. Not only should she have known he would bring Leila, but the terror filled her at facing Claude's mother was just as ridiculous.

Markus stared at her, concern etched across his features. "Are you all right?"

"*Oui*, I will be fine." The words tumbled out, though there was little conviction behind them.

"Sophie!" Bertrand bellowed at the door.

"In here, Papa."

Her father stormed into the room and grasped her hand, pulling her up into a crushing bear hug, squeezing so tight she let out a gasp and couldn't breathe.

When he set her back on her feet, she turned to Leila, who stood at his side like a ghost. Leila opened her arms, and with overflowing eyes, Sophie stepped into her embrace.

"You…" Sophie mumbled.

"You've lost weight," Leila whispered."

"You both have," Bertrand admonished, giving Leila the side-eye.

Heat rose up Sophie's neck. She didn't want to discuss her weight loss with her father. But seeing Leila's frail form reminded her Claude's absence had taken its toll on her mother-in-law as well. Shame filled her further as she thought about her initial reaction to hearing her voice outside. She dropped back into her chair.

"And you are?" Bertrand rounded on Markus like a bear protecting his cub.

"Markus, sir." Markus stood and shook her father's hand, unperturbed by his brusque manner. "I am a friend…"

Sophie's stomach dropped further. At this rate, she was going to need a shovel to get it off the floor.

"And you are here why?" Bertrand asked.

Leila placed a hand on his arm. Sophie gave her a tight smile of appreciation.

"I came to talk to Sophie. I was there with Claude… that day… I was with him and Sven…"

"Oh." Leila's single word came out as a squeak. Bertrand led her to an open chair and sat down in the empty chair next to hers.

"So, tell us what you know." Bertrand's no-nonsense demeanor took over at once.

Sophie was suddenly grateful for their presence. She knew what he was going to say and wished to the heavens she didn't have to hear it but knew she must.

"I'm so sorry, Sophie. I was too far away, and I didn't expect them to be swallowed by the waves."

Leila gasped and covered her mouth with the handkerchief gripped in her hand.

Sophie sat as Markus relayed what he had experienced the day of the tsunami when Claude had disappeared. Her teeth bit into her bottom lip so hard, she tasted the blood on her tongue.

Bertrand just nodded at Markus to continue. So, he did.

"When I saw the commotion on the beach, I knew something was wrong and motioned for them to come in. The last I looked back, Sven and Claude were paddling their crafts closer to the shore. The next thing I knew, something hit me from behind, my kayak was in the air, and I was upside down. I didn't realize it was a swell until I was underwater." He paused and reached for his glass of tea. The silence that surrounded them was crushing.

"I was close enough to the beach that people saw what had happened and pulled me to shore. If they hadn't, I wouldn't have made it. I didn't learn about Claude or Sven until I awoke the following morning in the clinic. I didn't know how to reach you, Sophie. I only had Sven's and Claude's mobile numbers, and I knew they had left their phones in their rucksacks at the kayak shack."

Sophie bobbed her head, unable to speak. It hurt to hear the words, but she had known for days her husband would have returned to her already if he had been able. As the words sank in, the last remaining thought that there was still a sliver of hope he'd return to her somehow evaporated.

"I told the doctors at the clinic if they came in, or if you came in, to call me. And I returned to Bali to tell Paige about Sven. They got busy, so it took them until this morning for me to learn where you were staying, and no news had come in about the guys."

Leila's gasps came harder as the tears slid down

her cheeks unhindered. Sophie wanted to crawl in a hole and hide.

Markus's voice was so forlorn, it left little room for doubt about his opinion as to the fate of her husband.

"I came as soon as I could get my hands on a vehicle and directions." He waved in the direction of the driveway.

Out of the corner of her eye, she could see a worn-out, single person moped sat just outside her front door. The bike had to be what he was referring to.

"And Paige? How is she?"

"She had to be sedated after I gave her the news. She flew home yesterday. She wanted to say goodbye, but she couldn't afford to wait any longer to return home to their children. She asked me to give you her number and have you call her when you were feeling up to it."

Sophie accepted the slip of paper and gave him a tight smile. Her stomach felt like she was spiraling down on a roller coaster. The weightlessness. The feeling like one was falling through the air—when the whole world disappeared beneath your seat— and for a moment, you were suspended in time and space.

A feeling she'd once reveled in, it had become a

constant companion, and now she hoped to never experience it again. The world she knew had slipped away beneath her feet, and her life had been derailed. Her mind stopped registering the rest of the conversation around her, blocking out all sound, though she continued to see everyone's lips move. She watched them through the unshed tears and fog that enveloped her brain.

This must have been how her father felt when he'd learned her mother was gone. The sense something was not right and would never be again. She'd weathered that storm because Claude held her hand and got her through it. He had been her rock. *And now, he too is gone.*

Sophie had to fight the urge to flee. All she wanted to do was escape this never-ending nightmare she was caught in.

CHAPTER 17

Going Home

Sophie

S ophie sat at the edge of the couch, a stubborn set to her shoulders, as she glared past her tears. "I'm not leaving without him," she said.

"*Fille tu ne peux pas rester!*" Bertrand said.

"Papa, please do not make me go. I cannot bear it."

Bertrand placed his hand on the back of her head. "Sophie. I'm so sorry, but he's gone. It's time to go home so we can properly mourn him."

Sophie glanced over at her mother-in-law. Leila sat with her hands folded in her lap. Her lips tightly pressed together as the tears streamed down her face. Sympathy coursed through her as she saw how crushed Leila was by the idea her only son, Claude, was gone forever.

Sophie's heart ached with a hollowness that had invaded her each morning. Addressing her mother-in-law, Sophie asked, "*Belle-mère*, do you want to leave?"

Leila's head popped up, and she wiped her tear-stained cheeks. Her voice trembled as she spoke. "*Non*, I do not want to go—"

"See, Papa—"

"But Bertrand is right. Claude is not coming back. If he were alive, he'd have moved heaven and earth to be by your side. You know this, Sophie. He would never leave you alone if he had a choice." Leila's body trembled as her hands covered her face, and she sobbed.

Sophie's shoulders slumped, defeated. If Claude's own mother believed him dead, she no longer had an ally to stand with her, and seeing Leila break down was more than she could handle.

"I need to lie down for a while. I don't feel well." She flew from the couch and made her way into her bedroom.

The inner strength she'd always counted on was fading fast. She felt like a shell of the person who had said her vows only three months before. A woman with endless possibilities in the palm of her hand, excited to face the future. But in the blink of an eye, the love of her life was gone, and she was left adrift in this world. Alone.

Her mobile phone vibrated across the nightstand as she reached the doorway. Shutting the door behind her, she picked it up, dropped onto the bed, and answered it.

"*Bonjour, mon amie.*"

"Sophie, how are you?"

"*Misérable.*" Sophie kicked off her shoes and wiggled her toes.

"Still no word on Claude?"

"Oh, Addy. What am I going to do? How can I be a widow after only being his wife for less than a month? I can't do this." Her voice dropped as the uncontrollable sobs wracked her body. After a moment, Addison's soft voice penetrated through her fugue state.

"We're all here for you, Sophie. You are stronger than you think, and you *will* get through this. We will be there at a moment's notice."

"Papa has talked me into going home. Though home will never be the same without Claude. But I can't stay in Bali anymore. There's nothing left for me here. It's been two months since the tsunami, and yesterday the government formally stated it is highly unlikely any of the remaining missing persons will be located. They've admitted there really is no hope of finding him."

"I'm so sorry, honey. Is there anything I can do?"

"*Non*, thank you. I just don't know how I'm going to face this world without him. He's been my best friend and my soulmate for more than half my life."

"I know, Soph. Be safe, and know I'm only a phone call away if you need anything."

"Give my love to the littles, and we'll talk soon."

"Love you, Sophie."

"Love you, too." Sophie ended the call and placed the phone back on the bedside table before sliding under the covers. With a heavy heart and a deep sigh, she closed her eyes and hoped for some momentary peace.

TWO HOURS PASSED, AND SHE WAS STILL STARING AT the ceiling. Lying there in the darkened room, she relived every moment of her life with Claude. The laughter, the fights, their adventures. When he looked at her with a mischievous glint. The way he loved her with his whole being. His gentle caresses, his passion.

Every time she stopped moving, the memories

flooded her mind. Her whole world had revolved around Claude since they were children. They played together, they learned to ride together. Other than the year she'd spent studying in Russia, they had been inseparable. There were very few memories throughout her entire life that didn't include him.

Deep in her gut, something told her she needed to stay, the pull was like an anchor to the island. But, two days later, unable to make further excuses, Sophie boarded her family's plane to return to France. Her heart and soul remained on the island, but her body trudged its way forward as expected.

CHAPTER 18

Unexpected Complications

Sophie

S ophie leaned her head against the cool wood of the vanity and curled her legs under her. Her entire body ached. For the fourth morning in a row, she'd heaved up everything in her stomach—long before breakfast had even been considered. Back in France for under a month, she still felt lost. She tried to rouse herself from going through the motions each day like a trained animal. Everyone treated her like a porcelain doll, afraid she might break or something.

Agnes called out from her bedroom. "*Madam*, I brought you some muffins."

"Ugh." The very idea of food made her stomach clench all over again.

"Are you ill again, *madam*?"

Sophie groaned as Agnes kneeled beside her on the marble floor and pressed a palm on her forehead. Flinching against the ice-cold hand on her warm brow, she hated to be called *madam*. Even though she was technically a married woman, it rankled to hear the term.

"You are dewy. But you have no fever. Shall I ring for the doctor?

Before Sophie could respond, her father's voice filled the room.

"Sophie, darling, you missed breakfast again. You can't keep holed up in your room forever," Bertrand said.

Sophie muttered expletives under her breath as Agnes laughed and tut-tutted her.

Bertrand rapped his knuckles on the bathroom door and called out again. "Sophie?"

"A moment please, *monsieur*," Agnes said.

"Agnes? Is everything all right?" Bertrand asked.

"Fine, fine. Let me get *madam* off the ground, and we'll be out shortly."

"Off the ground?" Bertrand's voice rose.

With a heave and a grunt, Agnes helped Sophie stand, though her legs were wobbly and opened the door.

"Papa, I'm fine," Sophie said as she leaned against the doorway.

"Soph, you need to go to the doctor. Honey, you've been sick for days."

"As I was telling her as well, *monsieur*," Agnes said.

"I'm fine, Papa, really," Sophie said.

"*Non*. You are not. Agnes, get her dressed. I'll call the doctor and have Hugo drive us in."

"Hello, I'm standing right here," Sophie huffed.

Agnes covered her mouth and turned her head, though her shaking shoulders gave away her amusement.

Bertrand chuckled as he stepped out of the room.

"Come now. Let's get you dressed comfortably," Agnes said.

AN HOUR LATER, SOPHIE SAT IN THE LOBBY OF their doctor's office, waiting. Her father refused to let her out of his sight, so he was beside her, flipping through a magazine and stealing glances at her. Though, when she turned her head, his gaze was always directed at the magazine in his lap.

When the nurse finally called her name, Bertrand started to stand, and Sophie pulled him back in his seat. "Papa, thank you, but I can do this on my own."

With a nod, Bertrand settled back into his seat and opened the magazine again. "I'll be right here waiting."

"I know, Papa. I know." She kissed his cheek and then walked across the lobby to follow the nurse.

She was alone in the doctor's room for only a moment before the doctor entered.

"Hello, Ms. Sophie. I am sorry for the many misfortunes that have befallen you since your beautiful wedding in the autumn." Dr. Bisset took Sophie's hand in hers.

Sophie bit her lip and nodded, afraid the words wouldn't get past the lump in her throat.

"So, what brings you to me today?"

"I have been ill for the last few days. Mornings, really. The rest of the day, I seem fine. It's when I first wake, I struggle with it. Then again, I've never been a morning person, to be honest." She gave a nonchalant shrug.

"Let me go ahead and have you fill this cup. The lavatory is across the hall. Leave it on the shelf, and we'll do a quick test."

Sophie nodded and took the cup with her as she stepped out of the exam room. She wasn't sure what a urine sample was going to tell the doctor about her stomach bug, but who was she to complain?

Five minutes later, she was back on the cold exam table, waiting for the diagnosis.

"When was your last cycle?"

"Cycle?" Sophie stared at the doctor, confused.

"Your period, Sophie. When was your last?"

"I don't know. I can't remember ..."

"I believe there's a possibility you're pregnant, my dear." The doctor looked over her clipboard. "We'll run the test to confirm, but I'm pretty sure that's what ails you."

"But I can't be. Claude is dead." And with that, the room spun and dropped her into a pool of blackness.

SOPHIE OPENED HER EYES, MOMENTARILY CONFUSED by the white tiles on the ceiling. Taking a deep breath, she could have sworn there were forget-me-nots nearby. *Where am I?* And then it clicked. She was seeing Dr. Bisset. But why was she lying down? And why was her father in the room having a hushed conversation with her doctor? She recalled leaving him in the lobby when the nurse took her back.

As she lifted her head up, the room got a little wavy. With a deep breath, she pushed herself into a sitting position. Her father and Dr. Bisset were so engrossed in whatever they were saying, neither had noticed her.

"Dr. Bisset?" Sophie hadn't intended it as a question, but that was how it sounded even to her ears.

"*Oui*, sorry, we were just discussing your options," Bertrand said.

"Options? I don't understand."

"The tests are back. You are pregnant. At least twelve weeks along," Dr. Bisset said.

The room started to spin again. The breakfast Sophie hadn't even eaten, just tasted for the benefit of Agnes, wanted to evacuate forcefully.

How had her life come to this? A wife. A widow. A single mother. In a matter of weeks. It was all too much to process.

Closing her eyes, she willed the contents of her stomach to stay put. So far, so good.

The doctor stared at her critically while her father patted her hand. "Sophie, you are going to need to start taking prenatal vitamins and stop drinking alcohol."

She was completely numb.

The doctor was talking to her, but her mind

couldn't reconcile the words. It was all gibberish to her.

Her father squeezed her hand. "Is there a specific brand, or is it a prescription?" he asked.

Looking from her father to the doctor, it was clear Sophie had missed something important, but she didn't care. "Is that all?" She directed her question to the doctor.

Dr. Bisset nodded. Sophie hopped down from the exam table and made her way to the door. Her hand on the knob, she turned and faced the doctor. "*Merci.*"

After pulling the door open, Sophie hurried out, not looking back. She needed air. Her lungs tightened like they would burst if she didn't get outside. She quickened her pace to the elevators. Glancing up at the lighted display, she saw the two elevators were sitting on other floors, nowhere near hers.

Panic filled her, and she stumbled her way over to the stairwell and shoved the door open. Her mind didn't register anything other than an instinctual flight response as she grabbed the handrail and fled down the steps.

Once she pushed open the last door, she wound her way through the dozens of people in the lobby to get out of the building. She came face to face with their chauffeur, Hugo, who rushed toward her.

"*Madam*? Is everything all right? Where is Mr. Compte?"

Her voice caught in her throat; she shook her head. Hugo gently took her arm and led her to the car. He opened the back door and set her on the edge of the seat, her legs still outside on the pavement. Then, he pulled a bottle of water from the pocket in the door and twisted the cap before pressing it into her hand.

She sipped the water as Hugo stared at her. His gaze was uncomfortable but full of concern.

"Sophie? Hugo? Is everything okay?" Bertrand asked as he stepped up to join them.

"*Oui*, sir. Ms. Sophie just needed some water and to catch her breath." Hugo winked at her as he stood to face her father.

Smiling at Hugo, silently thanking him for his discretion, she scooted over to make room in the car.

Her father held her hand as Hugo sped through the city. This left her to her whirling thoughts while lights danced across the window. On every corner, at every café, her mind played tricks on her, as she could have sworn she'd seen Claude. It was like a gut-punch every time.

When they reached the house, they retired to the library, and her father ordered tea, more to keep

Agnes from hovering than any real desire for the beverage. A few minutes later, Agnes brought a steaming ceramic pot and a tray of mugs. She settled them on the table while watching them through narrowed eyes before leaving the room. Sophie knew she was dying to know what the doctor said but would never ask.

Sophie wasn't in the mood for tea or conversation. Her mind was unable to fully grasp her new situation. It felt like some cruel cosmic joke. First, the loss of her husband and now the culmination of one of their dreams—come to pass after he was gone.

"Papa, I'm sorry, I'm exhausted. I'm going to take a bath before dinner."

"Sophie, please don't shut us out. You are not alone in all this."

"*Merci*, Papa. I just need time."

Without another word, she fled the parlor and raced up the stairs to her rooms. She couldn't handle any more side glances, or the tension that hung in the air with everyone's unspoken thoughts, concern etched across their faces.

A relaxing bath was what she needed. The fragrant bubbles were sure to calm her racing thoughts and ease the stiffness of her muscles. And she just needed some time alone where she didn't have to plaster the fake smile on her face, pretending like her world wasn't crashing down around her in flames.

TWO HOURS LATER, HER HAIR COMBED AND TWISTED on the top of her head, and a pair of jeans and sweater on, Sophie padded her bare feet down the stairs where she found her father and Leila sitting in the parlor sharing a pre-dinner drink. It took everything in her to keep one foot in front of the other. She didn't know how she was going to give the news to Leila and hoped her father had already done so to ease that burden.

Once they were seated around the dining table, Sophie reached deep inside for the courage to say what was eating away at her.

"I'd like to create a small plot at the farm with a headstone for Claude next to his father. A spot where I can place flowers on. To take his child to someday."

A hush descended around the room as if time itself stood still. She took a shaky breath, unsure what to say, to bring the conversation back to the table. Any conversation would be better than the oppressive silence.

"I understand. We will look into it and see what

we can come up with. Maybe a small garden and a bench, or even a fountain, if you'd prefer," Bertrand said.

Leila nodded, though she didn't offer up any opinions of her own. Sophie figured she was still in shock about the news of the baby. Her father would have invited Leila over for dinner for that purpose.

"And one more thing, if you don't mind. Can we wait until after the baby is born to declare him dead and have a funeral? If that's what you really want," Sophie said.

Leila stared at her. Her eyes glistened from the unshed tears pooled there.

Sophie sucked in a breath. It wasn't that she was trying to be insensitive, more that she was in over her head and didn't know the proper etiquette in situations such as this.

"Sure, why?" Bertrand asked.

"Because I just can't handle anything more at this point. The funeral would be the last step in accepting he's gone, and I just am not ready to put the last piece of the puzzle in place. I'm afraid, at this point, if I'm faced with any more shocks to the system, I'm going to lose this baby..." Sophie's words caught in her throat. "That somehow, some way, this last piece of Claude will be taken from me as well." She broke down as the sobs wracked her shoulders.

Leila reached over and covered her hand on the table with one of her own. "Oh, darling, of course, we will wait. We will bring this baby into the world first, and then we will say our goodbyes to Claude when you are ready."

"Thank you. I'm sorry, I know it's a lot to ask," Sophie said.

"You are my daughter, Sophie. And while I mourn the loss of my son, I would never want to cause you more pain. So, we wait. It is not too much to ask," Leila said.

Sophie wiped at the tears sliding down her face. Her heart ached for her mother-in-law and for her unborn baby who would never know their father. Her happily-ever-after was over, but she had to do everything in her power to stay strong now for their child. It was all that was left of what they'd shared.

CHAPTER 19

Rebuilding Communities

Sophie

Sophie hung as far back behind the large group scattered on the podium as was possible, wedged between her father and Leila. She was as big as a house and having so many people in close proximity made her twitchy. The baby was moving around again. This time, it felt like she was tap dancing against her ribs. So wrapped up in surviving the second trimester of her pregnancy, she hadn't paid much attention to the happenings taking place in the rest of the world. Since the death of the love of her life, her world had shrunk considerably. The morning sickness had just started to let up—even though the doctors had assured her it should have passed months before—it had hung on well into her sixth month.

The mayor of the island continued droning on. Sophie had long since stopped paying any attention to his speech. Instead, she took in the Physic Garden surrounding the clinic—it was breathtaking. She also searched the crowd gathered below for familiar faces. She hoped that she would have a chance to reconnect with the nurses that she'd worked so closely with after the earthquake and tsunami. The doctors were all there—of course, front and center—preening for the cameras as though they had any part in why her father had made such a generous donation to the island's medical clinic, bringing it into the twenty-first century.

The devastation to the island had been so great, their resources had been depleted long before they had a chance to get basic needs met. Electricity and clean water were the priorities. The roads were still a mess, and most businesses remained to limp along on bottled water and generated power. The clinic had begun sending people to Bali to be treated as their supplies were far below what was needed to care for everyone. That was when the nurses had sent her an email asking for support. By the time

Sophie had read it, her father had already sent them a sizable donation.

They appreciated such a large sum of money from a non-charitable organization so much they wanted to show their gratitude with a formal ceremony.

So, there she was. Returned to the island that held such heartbreak, expected to give a speech in front of hundreds of people all the while looking and feeling like the Goodyear Blimp.

"Now, it is my great honor and pleasure to introduce Mrs. Sophie Compte-Durand. The generous benefactor to our clinic and to our small island," the mayor said.

Her father patted her shoulder while Leila gave her hand a gentle squeeze. Sophie shook her head. She still wasn't quite sure how she got talked into being the face of this whole thing. Stepping up to the podium, she shook the mayor's extended hand.

"Thank you, Mr. Komar. We are thankful to you for all you have done. And we are proud to be a part of it."

Turning to the crowd below, she took one more deep breath and smiled, sniffing back the tears threatening to spill down her cheeks.

"Thank you for the warm welcome. Six months ago, I came to this island as a newlywed, and a short two months later, I left it as a widow. Like many of you, I continue to mourn the loss of a loved one."

She rubbed her protruding belly in gentle circles, trying to calm herself, so as not to agitate the baby further from her increasing stress. The water feature in the garden—a teak bridge, joining the rockery and the botanical plants, over a small waterway filled with lotus flowers—calming movement focused her.

"I am reminded life goes on, and so must we. I hope the new clinic will be able to bring much-needed care to this wonderful community. And this memorial will honor the loved ones we still hold dear to our hearts, as well as the survivors."

Her hands shook as she flipped through the small cards. Setting the cards down, her fingers clenched around them, and she turned her attention back to the people.

"Thank you for all you did for me and each other. I am proud to have been a part of those first days when everyone pulled together to help."

Looking at the many faces staring up at her, she noticed the small group of nurses standing on the outskirts of the group, a slight distance from where the doctors stood front and center. When the women caught her eye, they each waved at her. She smiled and gave them a slight nod to let them know she'd seen them.

Sophie took a step back and shook the mayor's hand again before slipping back into the group. Her father and Leila helped her down from the dais and walked with her to greet the small group of nurses she considered friends. This was the only part of returning to the island that held any pleasure for her.

CHAPTER 20

Revelations

Sébastien

Sébastien trudged his worn and weary body through the back door. After a day of clearing an old schoolyard, he was spent. The air conditioner was blasting its frigid air to combat the outside temperatures, and the house was blessedly silent. Just what he needed after a long day baking under the unforgiving sun. That, and a shower. Sniffing his shirt, he drew his head back and winced. *Yeah, a shower is in order.*

He dropped his plastic lunch cooler on the counter and made his way into the master bedroom.

The cold water flowed over his head and down

his back, taking with it the tree sap and sweat covering his body. His warmed skin cooled to a more comfortable temperature, and his stiff muscles relaxed. After staying in a little longer than usual, he stepped out and threw on a pair of shorts and a T-shirt.

The voices of his girlfriend and her brother drifted into the room, informing him he was no longer alone, and the raised tones implied the blessed peace was gone as well.

"Anisah, you have to come clean," Basuki said.

"This is stupid. Why couldn't you just leave well enough alone? You had to go and ruin everything," she hollered back.

"Sit," Basuki responded.

Sébastien paused at the edge of the kitchen. Anisah dropped into the chair next to her brother like a petulant child. Her arms were crossed, and her expression mutinous.

"If you don't tell him, I will."

"You've told everyone else. Why haven't you?"

Sébastien was taken aback by her hostility. He'd never seen her be anything but calm and gentle. And he'd never known the siblings to fight like this. The hair on the back of his neck prickled.

"Anisah, stop it. You are only making it worse. You owe him the truth."

Sébastien came in and took a seat across from the siblings.

Anisah bowed her head and reached for Sébastien's hand. The tension in the room was palpable as her hand trembled in his. The volleying of barbs between Anisah and Basuki further confused him. This was unusual, and clearly, whatever the problem was, it had him smack dab in the middle of it.

Sébastien sat at the table across from, Anisah, as tears slid down her cheeks. Basuki, his only other friend in the world, sat beside her, scowling.

"I have something I have to tell you, and I'm not sure how or where to even start. Please don't be angry with me."

"Of course, I won't be angry. Talk to me." He caressed the back of her hand with his thumb. Her obvious distress and Basuki's blatant irritation made his gut clench tighter.

"Well…" The words flowed from her mouth like a raging river. Once she started, she didn't stop to even take a breath.

He shook his head, dumbfounded that anyone could talk that long without breathing. And try as he might, he couldn't understand what he was hearing. There was little room for doubt the tale was true, considering the expressions on their faces. But it made no sense.

On the one hand, it was good to have an identity again, to know who he was—well, at least be told who he was. He still had zero recollection of anything other than waking up on a cot in a makeshift clinic nearly four months ago. Anisah had been there when he awoke, bathing his face and talking to him.

The doctors and nursing staff had informed him how he had arrived. Surfers had found him unconscious and alone on the beach during their usual sunrise ritual and brought him to the clinic. No one knew his name, where he'd been staying, or where he'd come from. No one could explain how he'd wound up on the beach in a wetsuit.

After three weeks, in what amounted to the small local hospital, he was released with a broken collarbone, broken leg, and a dislocated shoulder. He had been kept longer than usual because he had to have surgery on his collarbone—which had to wait until after his head injury had resolved. It turned out to be a concussion, but the MRIs hadn't discovered any long-term brain damage, though, his memory had not returned, even after he had healed. Anisah and her brother offered him a place to stay with them while he recovered, and the authorities continued to search for his identity though they had made it clear they didn't expect to learn much. Since he had no money and nowhere else to go, he'd accepted.

They had settled into a routine—him helping around the house while Anisah went to the clinic each day and Basuki to his landscaping job. Once his body had healed enough for him to be mobile for longer periods, he joined Basuki outside, doing basic lawn maintenance. It appeared he had a knack for working with his hands.

"Sébastien, I'm so sorry. I should have told you sooner," Anisah cried.

"Apparently, my name is Claude," he whispered.

"Yes, yes, Claude. I'm sorry."

"I don't understand why you would keep this a secret for so long."

"She was wrong," Basuki said. He gave his sister a sidelong glance.

"Yes, I was wrong. I was afraid I would lose you," Anisah whispered.

"You knew I had a family. A wife. How could you not tell me? They have thought I was dead for months. I've been struggling to figure out who I am, and all this time, you knew."

His heart thumped, angry in his chest. He felt the blood race up his neck and to his face, heating it as it went. The lump in his throat constricted his breathing, while the rock in his stomach grew to feel like a hundred-pound boulder crushing his intestines. His mind raced with all the implications.

"No. Only the last few weeks. Your picture was on the television during the opening of a new clinic on Nusa Penida. A memorial clinic for those lost during the earthquake and tsunami. No one considered you had traveled so far, so no one thought to reach out to Nusa Penida or Bali. We all assumed you'd come from Lombok, though no one recognized you from there."

Basuki put his hand on his sister's. "I've talked to the authorities in Bali. They've informed your family. They'll be here in the morning."

Anisah continued to sob as Basuki spoke.

"Here? I'm not sure I can face them," Claude said. His emotions were raw. His gut churned. Anisah avoided looking at him, which only made the moment much more painful.

"I understand. They have been made aware of the situation and were told you have no memory."

"Thank you."

Anisah jumped to her feet, knocking the chair

over as she stood and rushed out of the small kitchen, and then the bedroom door slammed.

"Claude, we are both so sorry for what you've gone through. You have become a part of our small family, and Anisah loves you."

"Why couldn't she trust me enough to tell me?"

"You and I both know the answer to that. You have a wife, a family, and a career waiting for you. Whether or not you remember any of it now, it doesn't change the fact you belong somewhere else, to someone else. Anisah knew she would have to let you go. We both did."

"Do you hate me for that?" Claude asked.

"Of course not, bro. None of this is your fault. It's unexpected, and it sucks, but it's the right thing to do, and we all have to accept it."

"Thank you. I wish I could say I understand, but it's all so overwhelming right now."

"Give it time. Maybe once you get home and are in familiar surroundings, your memory will come back."

Claude nodded, but he wasn't sure what to expect. *I have a wife.* His head throbbed as these thoughts swirled, bouncing around. *I'm a veterinarian at a horse farm.* His wife's family farm, it would seem.

Claude pushed his chair back and stood. "I need

some air. I'm sorry. I just can't wrap my head around this." Claude walked out to the garden, leaving Basuki at the table, and Anisah—he assumed —still in the bedroom since she had not returned to the kitchen. For months, he'd wondered why he wasn't fully connected to Anisah, assuming the loss of his memories and doubt of who he was, had been the sole reason. Claude wondered if his heart always knew it belonged to someone else. The thought of facing his wife tomorrow made his pulse race. Could she forgive him for the fact that he broke his vows?

The idea that he was a veterinarian was an interesting piece of his identity puzzle. He liked working outdoors and with his hands, which was why he had worked so well in Basuki's business. But a horse farm—a breeding farm no less—was a different story. Not that he didn't like animals; he just couldn't imagine that was where his passion lay.

Claude hated to leave things like they were with Anisah, but didn't know how to fix things, either— because he *was* going. Of that, there was no doubt. The uncertainty that had plagued him the last few months only seemed to solidify in his stomach now that he had a name and a job. He had a wife and a whole other life that didn't include the small island he'd grown to love. It was so surreal. A part of him questioned it all. But the way Anisah had reacted made it clear, at least they believed it to be true. He was going to miss it there, and while Claude still didn't know who he was or where he came from, others did. They knew where he belonged, and they would be taking him home.

Wherever that is.

CHAPTER 21

Force of Reckoning

Sébast-Claude

Sébast-Claude stood there, frozen in place. Peering across the parking lot, he watched a young woman surrounded by an entire entourage step off the boat and walk across the dock.

Basuki had driven him into town to the ferry station. Anisah hadn't said another word to him. She hadn't emerged from their bedroom the night before, and then she left this morning without saying good-bye before the sun had reached the horizon. He'd heard the click of the front door closing, and before he'd managed to untangle himself from the blankets on the couch where he'd spent the night, her car was pulling out of the driveway.

It sliced another gash through his soul, knowing she wouldn't face him. He hated causing her such pain. She didn't deserve any of this. Anisah and her brother had been nothing but good to him, a complete stranger to them. She was a good woman who should be loved by someone who could be her everything. It wasn't him, but it didn't mean he wanted to see her hurt or be the reason she was hurting.

Basuki nudged him, pulling his attention back to the group of people coming closer. An older couple and he caught a slight glimpse of a younger woman trailing behind them. It had to be his wife. The sudden urge to flee, to escape, invaded his usual composure. His pulse raced, and his nerves hummed under his skin. As they approached, the tension in the air grew thicker.

Finally, they stood before him. It seemed like it'd taken forever for them to cross the dock and reach the pavilion where he stood. The older man extended his hand. Claude reached out in response.

"Hi, I'm Sébastien," he said without thinking.

The man's brow cocked, and the older woman standing next to him gasped.

"I'm sorry. It's Claude. I just learned this yesterday, so please bear with me as I adjust to all the changes!" he said.

"It's okay, son. We will face this challenge together," the man said.

The older woman stepped forward and wrapped him in a tight embrace, sobbing. Confused and unsure what to expect, he stood there stiff as a board and patted her back.

After a few awkward moments, she released him and stroked his cheek. As she took a step back, she spoke something in another language and then quickly apologized.

"What language was that?" he asked. He was sure he should know it, but the words were all Greek to him.

"French," the older woman said.

"He doesn't remember he speaks French?" the young woman said. "*Merde.*"

"Patience, *ma petit fille*," the man spoke.

He watched their interaction, not understanding any of the words, but getting the gist of the conversation all the same.

"This is my friend, Basuki," Sébast-Claude said. He didn't know what else to say and wanted to break the uncomfortable tension.

Basuki shook everyone's hand as they introduced themselves to him.

He learned the older couple were not a couple at all, and the woman was actually his mother, not his wife's mother. He wondered where his father was and his wife's mother. *Interesting.*

The young woman moved to the side, giving him a better look at her

Exquisite. There was no other word for the beautiful creature standing there. She was like a delicate flower.

Basuki's eyes grew wide as he shook Sophie's trembling hand. It was replaced lightning-fast, however, as Sébast-Claude took in her condition.

"You're pregnant?" he blurted out.

"*Oui.* Just over seven months, now," she said. Her hand stroked her stomach bump as she spoke.

He could tell it was a subconscious reaction, that she wasn't even thinking of what her hand was doing.

"How can this be?" he asked.

"We were married for over three weeks before you disappeared," she responded with a knowing look. "And together many times before that."

He could feel annoyance coming off her in waves. He didn't know why she was so upset with him. Then again, it wasn't like he would know if he *had* done something wrong.

Shame flooded through him as he stared at her protruding belly. He could only imagine the hell she had gone through, thinking she was a widow, learning she was going to have a child—his child—and expecting to have to raise it alone.

He sucked in a deep breath. *I'm going to be a father.* She had been navigating it all without him, while he had been living a relatively comfortable existence with Basuki and Anisah. How would she ever be able to forgive him? How could he forgive himself? Not knowing didn't absolve him for his failings, in his opinion.

He stood frozen, gaping at her like a dumb-struck teenager.

What should I do now? Do I kiss her? Shake her hand? Hug her?

What was the appropriate greeting for a pregnant wife you didn't know?

So, he stared at her like a confused puppy.

Basuki coughed, and everyone's attention turned to him.

"Sébast—sorry. Claude. I will go now and let you get to know your family. You have our—my number, please keep in touch. Let me know you've settled in and are doing well."

There was no hesitation as Claude hugged him. Basuki had been his brother for the last few months, there was little doubt this would be the last time they saw each other. While a part of him died at the thought of cutting these ties, he couldn't do further harm to these people who had taken such good care of him when he had nothing to give them in return.

Claude doubted he'd ever find the words to explain Anisah and Basuki, and everything they meant to him, to his wife and family. And reaching out to them, to talk about a life they would never be a part of, wouldn't be fair to them, either.

He held onto Basuki longer than one would expect when two men embrace. But this was a goodbye he wasn't quite ready for.

Basuki patted his arm, and, with one last shake of everyone's hand, he said his goodbyes and left.

Sébast-Claude sniffed back the tears that welled up, refusing to break down in front of these strangers.

"Claude?" the man asked.

"Yes, sir?"

"If you are ready, let's take the ferry back to Bali. Our plane is waiting for us there to take you home."

"Your plane?" Sébast-Claude asked.

Just how rich are these people?

"Yes, our company plane is sitting in Bali."

Sébast-Claude nodded. He had no words, though he was full of questions. He was unsure how they would be received so, he remained silent.

Bertrand wrapped his arm around Sophie and

led her down the path back to the dock, leaving him with his mother. He slipped the knapsack over his shoulder and lent her an elbow.

She slipped her arm through his and kept up a light chatter about their life on the farm as they walked to the waiting boat.

Four hours later, they stepped off the boat and loaded into a car that took them to the airport.

Stepping out of the sedan, his vision was filled with a modest-sized jet. The words *Dassault Falcon 900B* were printed on the side of the plane, near the back fin. The aircraft was magnificent. It was sleek on the outside, with glossy white and blue pinstripes down the sides. He was the last to enter the plane as he had to pause at the entryway to take a breath. Inside, there was a cabin with twelve large, leather, reclining seats.

It was all overwhelming. Sébast-Claude took the seat next to his mother without thinking much about it. It hadn't occurred to him to sit next to Sophie until he caught her staring at him. He felt like he was a new student at a school play yard and had made a mistake. Unsure, insecure, and fumbling his way through his first day, he couldn't remember feeling this nervous in his life.

Hell, who am I kidding? I can't remember anything about *my life. Maybe I've always been like this.*

Sébast-Claude sat as his mother talked about memories he didn't recall, people he didn't know, and a language he couldn't speak.

But she seemed unconcerned as she prattled away. Every once in a while, he glanced up and watched Sophie turn her face in another direction to avoid his gaze. The tension was almost painful. Just as his gut felt twisted in knots at all the changes the last two days had brought with them.

It stung a little, though. Deep down, he knew her reluctance to face him was just as much as his was to face her. He hadn't been very warm and forthcoming, and she had every reason to feel like she was on an emotional rollercoaster.

If she ever learned the truth of his life in the last few months, it would only push her farther away from him. He didn't know her, but he also didn't want to see her hurt anymore because of him, either. There was no doubt she'd suffered enough. It was etched in the creases around her eyes and the tightness of her lips.

CHAPTER 22

A Shock to the System

Sophie

Sophie stood slightly behind her father, using him as a human shield. There was no denying she was behaving like a coward. Though, considering she had been anxious and experiencing panic attacks for most of the past twenty-four hours, there had to be some allowances made. One could even blame her behavior on her raging hormones and delicate condition if they were so inclined.

Nevertheless, she was still in a state of disbelief. Her husband was alive and standing, not even ten feet away from her. It wasn't a mistake or some cosmic joke. Claude was real, though he looked much darker than he had a few months ago.

Though always an outdoorsman, clearly he had spent plenty of time in the Indonesian sun. Yet, in so many ways, he appeared the same. The familiar strength and stature were still there—that regal bearing she'd always admired.

All she had been told was that he had been found on a beach near the northwest side of Lombok Island, on one of the Gili Islands. Considering the confusion, no one had expected him to wash that far north of where he had been last seen, near the coast of Penida, so no one thought to look there.

While the authorities in Bali were convinced he had perished at sea, the people on Gili Air had assumed he had come from Lombok Island. And of course, there had been no communication between the islands to change any of these assumptions.

What she hadn't been told, but had overheard between her father and Leila the night before, was that Claude had been living with a woman and her brother for the last few months.

Cold sweat had dripped down her neck between her shoulder blades, pulling her from her zombie state. Knowing her father and Claude's mother had no intention of sharing this bit of information with her left her torn.

She wanted to confront them. The anger

burning inside of her wanted its pound of flesh. She had spent months grieving, had many sleepless nights in an empty bed. Puking her guts out every morning because of the pregnancy, which had been far rougher than she ever thought possible. The doctors assured her she was fine—though uncomfortable, she was healthy, as was the baby. Though she hadn't felt that way each morning as she tossed her cookies. She had pledged her life to this man and had honored those vows even after everyone had told her he was dead. And to hear he'd been living a grand new life, with another woman, was like a knife in the heart. With a slight bump on the head, he could move on and start an entirely new life without looking back.

Who does that?

She was gutted. She had loved him all her life. Loved him when they were together and loved him when she thought he was gone. The unfairness of it all ripped her heart to shreds. While infidelity was a common occurrence in her culture, Sophie had never expected to experience it herself. An overwhelming jealousy, she never considered herself capable of, reared its ugly head. The green-eyed monster raged through her. Cutting her deep and tearing her apart.

Standing there, watching him talk to her father

without a care in the world—God, she wanted to slap someone. Scream at him for leaving her and starting fresh. It took every ounce of willpower she owned to stand behind her father and bite her tongue. Oh, how she longed to lash out. But it would do no good. It would only upset her father and Leila more, and they were already more than worried enough about her and the baby.

CHAPTER 23

Letting Go

Sophie

S ophie closed her eyes and sucked in a deep breath. She ignored the look she was getting from him. At this point, it was all she could do to not slap him silly. *Breathe. Just breathe…*

But it was getting harder each day to hide her disappointment and growing frustration with how things were between her and her returned-from-the-dead husband.

He now slept in her father's guest room every night, a few doors down from her suite of rooms. Deep down, she knew she should feel grateful—at least he was now living under the same roof as her.

For the first few weeks after they returned to France, he had stayed at his mother's house. While they had not gotten around to discussing the exact plan for where they would live after they returned from their honeymoon, she assumed they would stay with her father in the apartment in the city until they had the opportunity to find a home of their own. Together.

Nothing had worked out as expected.

She felt just as lost and confused, having him home—alive—as she had for the months she had lived with the knowledge that he was gone.

Claude had given her no encouragement. No hope their future would be as they had always planned. Each day they co-existed like roommates, not even as friends. At least friends communicated. They talked. They laughed. They enjoyed being in each other's presence.

He didn't ignore her, as much as avoid her whenever possible, without being obvious about it. Claude went to the farm each day, taking his meals with his mother instead of at the main house. Most of his time was spent in the stables with Eddie, or with their old on-call veterinarian who came each afternoon to tutor Claude until he felt comfortable again as a trained vet.

The last trimester of her pregnancy was just as uncomfortable and miserable as the first and second ones had been. Sick every morning, she couldn't get comfortable no matter what position she sat in. Sleep was near impossible. Her moods were in-flux, and her temper short.

The strain of the lack of improvement with her marriage only added to the overall feeling of restlessness invading her mind. Her father told her time was all that was needed for things to return to normal. Leila had cautioned her patience was the only way to reach Claude. Everyone who knew them and loved them all came with their own nuggets of advice.

While she was grateful for their love and support, none of their suggestions made a difference. Making his favorite foods, watching his favorite movies. His favorite shirt, or book, or music. His mother had told him stories of his childhood, he'd watched home movies of life on the farm. Nothing had brought any glimmer of recognition to the surface.

Claude remained physically present while a million miles away emotionally. It gutted her. She was quickly losing faith things would ever be restored. Sophie had no idea what Claude was thinking or feeling—which made it harder to gauge where things stood.

The tension between them tore her up inside. This should be one of the happiest moments of their lives. Planning on having a child together and the building of their family. Yet, Claude still hesitated to touch her. When she hugged him, he stood there stiff as a board and just draped an arm around her. He never actually embraced her, and his kisses were chaste, like those he gave his mother.

Sophie doubted their marriage would survive. She had no choice but to hold on until the baby was born, but if Claude didn't want to remain married after that, she would set him free. A black void filled her soul at the idea of walking away from him, but she couldn't keep hoping for her old life back if that wasn't what he wanted. It wasn't fair to either of them.

Her hand trembled as she stroked her belly, rubbing it in small circles to let her daughter know she was there. The baby nudged her from within in response.

Sophie sniffed back the tears threatening to spill. The crack in her heart widened a little more each day. She felt like she was grieving for her husband all over again. Just how many times was she expected to say goodbye and mourn her lost dreams? She didn't think she had much left in her to keep fighting this losing battle.

"Are you okay?"

The question startled her, pulling her from her reverie.

"I'm sorry, what was that?" she asked.

"I asked if you were doing okay," Claude said.

"*Oui*. Just thinking of the baby. She's moving around a bit. Would you like to feel?" She already knew the answer but felt obligated to offer him the chance to participate in the experience.

"*Non*, that's okay." Claude waved his hand in the air as he took a step back.

Her heart sank at his lack of interest in their baby.

"The property is nice. It's not like Lombok island, and the weather is different, but the flowers are beautiful here, too. There's this little garden in the back of the house, it's got these little sprockets of forget-me-nots in the corner—"

A little glimmer of hope creeped into her heart. Maybe their flowers would bring his memories back. She would grasp at anything that might change things between them.

"Ah, Sophie, darling, there you are," Bertrand called out from the doorway.

"*Bonjour*, Papa."

"Claude," Bertrand said. He clapped Claude on the shoulder and leaned in. "Is my grand-daughter kicking again?"

"*Oui*, I think she's playing football in there." Sophie rubbed her stomach again.

"May I?" her father asked.

At her nod, he reached over, rubbed her belly, and crooned. "Are you getting restless in there, little one? Soon, *ma cherie*."

Sophie laughed. As she glanced up at Claude, her breath caught in her throat as he looked away. A coldness seeped into her gut at Claude's dismissal. He wasn't even pretending to be interested for the sake of appearances. He really didn't care about her or their child.

"Well, I'll leave you and head back to the stables." Claude left, the door clapping against the frame in his haste.

Sophie let out a strangled moan.

"Ah, darling, give him time. This is an adjustment for him."

"And for me too, Papa—and yet you don't see *me* avoiding *him* every chance I get."

"True. Chin up. I have faith your patience shall be rewarded in time."

Sophie rolled her eyes and looked away. She wasn't going to argue her feelings with her father. If he was convinced all would be well in time, nothing would change his mind.

CHAPTER 24

Missteps Abound

Claude

Claude froze, dumbstruck when Sophie asked him if he wanted to touch her stomach. Though he was curious to know what she experienced when her eyes lit up and her expression changed from concentration to awe.

However, the idea of touching her scared the living hell out of him. It shouldn't. She was his wife, after all. But it didn't feel that way. They felt more like strangers than husband and wife. The awkward tension that hung between them whenever they were in the same room together was suffocating. His breath often caught in a lump in his throat, and all rational thoughts fled from his mind as sheer terror consumed him.

It stung when he saw the disappointment flash in her eyes when he turned her down. She didn't say anything, would only nod or turn her attention in another direction, no longer looking at him. The air surrounding her only chilled further each time it happened.

Shame filled him, knowing he hurt her by not being more attentive. He should participate more, assist her more, show more enthusiasm or interest in her condition. Yet, his gut instinct wasn't to reach out as much as it was to retreat.

There was this moment when they were talking that made him feel connected. It wasn't about the baby—which seemed like it should be the strongest link they share—but about silly flowers. Why would tiny blue flowers make her eyes light up and a wistful expression flit across her face? He shook his head. It didn't make sense.

Claude wished he could explain the warring thoughts and emotions that collided in his brain. He knew he was handling it all wrong. There didn't seem to be the right way to handle it, though. For months, his mother had filled him in on his childhood relationship with Sophie, how they had always been inseparable, and how that relationship grew until they married the year before.

He still couldn't wrap his head around being a husband, and, very soon, a father as well. It wasn't that he loathed the idea—more a foreign concept to him. In his previous life, he was sure he'd probably given the matter plenty of thought and consideration. But for the life of him, he just couldn't picture any of it.

It wasn't because he didn't want to. Or that he wasn't open to the idea. Claude just couldn't seem to make it compute into his consciousness. This only made it so much harder to relate to Sophie as his wife and the mother of his unborn child.

Everyone had been patient and considerate of his situation from the very beginning. But he knew this wouldn't last if things didn't change. Eventually, the expectation was that he would remember and pick up the pieces of his life from before would rear its ugly head.

CLAUDE NEEDED TO ESCAPE THE ROOM SOPHIE WAS laboring in. It bothered him, for reasons he had yet to fully explore, to see her in distress. She was still a new person to him—essentially a stranger, but it was beginning to feel like she hadn't always been. It was inexplicable. It might be the history and stories he had been inundated with since his return, or something deeper, something more. He still wasn't sure. As Claude sat and watched Sergei expertly wrangle, and mostly entertain his two children in the waiting room, an unexpected, yet faintly familiar longing began expanding in his chest. The feeling continued to swell until he could hardly breathe—like a small elephant had taken up residence on his chest. *I want this*. Had wanted it. Still wanted it. The whole deal. Wife. Children. Family. The familiarity told him it wasn't a new feeling. It was something that had come into being long before the wedding and honeymoon he still could not remember. But did that fact really matter? He may not remember anything concrete yet, but that didn't mean he couldn't learn it over again, did it? He could choose all of it, couldn't he?

He wondered if he and Sophie had ever discussed names for children they might someday have. What kind of name might he have chosen? Glancing again at Sergei and then the children, the answer entered his mind unbidden. *They named their children after their parents.* Well, that might be something. Especially since, memory or no, it was something Sophie and he seemed to share, the loss of a parent. A boy might have his father's name in some part, a girl her mother's. But what had it been? He went back over the stories and histories in his mind, so recently related to him, but didn't think it had been mentioned. The concentration made his temples ache, so he relented, intending to put a pin in it for later. But as he let it go, it surfaced on its own from the void. *Nadeen. Sophie's mother's name was Nadeen.* It wasn't much, just a name and a feeling, but it felt like a glimmer of sunshine in the dead of night. He hoped everyone else would view it the same.

CHAPTER 25

A Pleasant Surprise

Sophie

S ophie had been in labor for more than twenty-four hours. The entire process, from the morning before, had been an aggravatingly slow build-up. She'd walked and danced and taken a hot bath. Even eaten incredibly spicy Thai food for dinner the night before. Yet, nothing worked. Her body refused to cooperate, and it was taking its toll on everyone's patience.

They'd arrived at the hospital before dawn when her water broke, and yet the labor had not progressed. The doctor assured her it was normal, but she didn't care. She was ready to evict the interloper, and she didn't care whether her daughter agreed or not.

Addison stood off to the side of her bed, smoothing the hair from her forehead, next to Agnes, Marte, and Leila on her left. Her father and her husband hovered over her on the right. The room felt like it was shrinking, and every time someone new walked in, she thought she was going to scream.

Bertrand and Claude stepped out often to join Sergei in the waiting room, leaving just the women to cluck and fuss, which rubbed her nerves even more raw.

"You will be fine, honey. It's no different than birthing a horse," Addison said. She wiped a cool cloth across Sophie's forehead.

"What are you trying to say? That I have a horse!" Sophie hissed.

"No, of course not."

"Well, it feels like it every time she kicks," Sophie muttered through clenched teeth as another contraction tore through her.

Addison laughed. "I'm saying you know better than anyone, that it just takes time and patience. So, relax and suck on these ice chips."

Sophie grunted. "I need more than ice. Where's the doctor? I need that damn epidural now!"

The anesthesiologist chuckled as he walked in. "You called."

"Yes, I need… oh, you brought it," Sophie said.

"I did. Let me check your status, and then we can proceed." He popped his head under the sheet and back out again, making sure she was covered before he patted her knee. "You've reached six centimeters, so you are ready. Now, roll over and hold still, and I'll make it all better."

Sophie did as she was told. She wasn't shy about not liking the pain, and she had no intention of doing this without all the help she could get.

Twenty minutes later, the epidural kicked in and took the edge off the pain. It was still there, but it didn't feel as though she was being ripped apart from the inside out any longer.

It also eased a little of her frustration. She was so over being pregnant and more than ready to meet her daughter and have her body back.

The epidural did the trick. While getting to six centimeters had taken half the day, the last four seemed to speed past in no time. Not that the drug had actually done anything to move her dilation along, more she wasn't in so much agony that each moment was noted in exacting detail. She was far more comfortable and easily distracted by her family.

"Okay, now. Everyone out," the nurse ushered everyone out of the room.

"Except you." Leila snagged Claude's shirtsleeve.

The nurse giggled at the blush spreading across Claude's cheeks.

With everyone out of the room, the doctor swept in and sat down on the waiting chair at the foot of the bed. She took a quick peek under the sheet covering her lower half.

"Looks like it's time. Are you ready for this?"

"I think it might be a little late to change my mind, Doc," Sophie muttered through her clenched teeth.

With a laugh, she patted her knee. "So it is. Okay, then. Let's bring this baby into the world."

Two long and laborious hours later, Sophie sucked in a deep breath and then pushed with the last of her strength. A few moments later, the baby was whisked away, and her vitals checked before the doctor laid her daughter on her chest.

The little squirmer reached her tiny fingers up and grasped a tendril of Sophie's sodden strands of hair. Her eyes closed, and her face scrunched up as her bottom lip twitched with each breath filling Sophie's heart with a sense of joy that had been absent for far too long.

One nurse took the baby to do all the baby stuff like measurements and another helped clean her up while Claude stepped out to tell their family about the baby.

Twenty minutes later, tearing her gaze from her daughter's face, she smiled as the nurse let her family back into the room. Claude returned moments later with a pot of forget-me-nots in his hands.

Her heart swelled at this simple gesture.

"And what is this precious child's name?" Marte asked.

"Adryanna," Sophie said. She nuzzled the little button nose of the warm bundle in her arms.

"How about Nadeen for her middle name? After your mother," Claude said.

A hush fell over the room, like a dense fog, as everyone turned to look at Claude.

"Claude?" Sophie's voice was barely audible.

"Yes, darling?"

Sophie held her breath. The way he said it, it was like he was the old Claude. It wasn't the words, more the inflection in his voice. There was a reverence there she hadn't heard since their honeymoon.

There was a twinkle in his eye as he held her hand and stroked their daughter's cheek with his finger.

She looked over at her father, the tears pooling in his eyes, and she smiled.

"That is a beautiful gesture, Sophie," Bertrand said.

"Yes, it is, Papa. But it's not mine."

Bertrand swiped at his eyes. "I don't understand?"

"Claude and I never got as far as middle names. And I don't recall ever discussing Mama's name at all. Leila?"

"*Non*, we never discussed names, either. Claude and I have talked about his late papa and his childhood, with you, of course, but I never mentioned your family. I thought I'd leave that to you out of respect."

Bertrand turned to Claude. As everyone continued to stare at him, the scrutiny was making him visibly fidget. "Claude, what made you think of Nadeen?"

"I wish my papa and Sophie's mama could have been here to see us all grown. To see us marry, to see our beautiful daughter born. To see how strong her daughter has had to be through so much sorrow and tragedy. I thought this might bring a bit of her into our new lives since she isn't."

Sophie's chest tightened as she struggled for air. She hadn't expected such a sentiment from Claude, who, since his return from the islands, had been mostly aloof and distant. No matter what she said or did to reach the man she once knew, nothing worked. The months had sped by, and they were still strangers. The man she had married less than a year before had left her sitting by the pool one day and had disappeared. He was back, physically at least, though his memories and his love for her had remained absent.

"I recalled Addison and Sergei had named their children after their parents and thought Sophie might like to do the same."

"That was very thoughtful," Bertrand said.

"Maybe we could name our son after my papa?"

Sophie burst into tears. A quick glance had her seeing tears roll down Leila's cheeks as she gripped Marte's hand. It was completely plausible Claude would consider their late parents. She didn't need to read any more into it.

Agnes stood shaking and clasping Marte's other hand. The baby wailed.

Claude reached over and roughed her nose. "May I?"

"Of course."

"Come here, princess. No more tears. Today is a happy day. It's full of families, and it's full of love." Claude nuzzled her neck and crooned softly. He began humming a lullaby that was a favorite of her mother's, who often sang them to sleep as children.

Everyone in the room stood in silent shock as the realization that at least some of Claude's memories had returned reached each of them in turn.

Making Memories

EPILOGUE

One Year Later
Sophie

S ophie passed through the kitchen and looked over at the tousled hair of her daughter and goddaughter. They were celebrating her daughter's first birthday. Bertrand and Claude had asked if they could keep the festivities minimal. Just family, the members of the farm, and Addison's family, of course. Leila, Marte, and Agnes reluctantly agreed. Though they thought it should be a party to be remembered.

So, of course, they compromised. It was all that and then some, with the best food and delicacies available, but the guest list had remained small and intimate.

Adryanna and Natalya giggled and waved dirty hands at Sophie as she headed up the back steps to the office above. Shaking her head, she smiled. The girls were already covered in something sticky, while Maxim was in the stables with Claude and Sergei.

As she walked into her third-floor office, Addison was already sitting at Claude's desk, papers spread out across the surface, grading her student's midterm assignments. As tenured professors at the university, she and Sergei were always inundated with work.

"How do the essays look?" Sophie asked.

"They have improved since last semester, to be sure. What are the girls doing?"

"Getting sticky. They will need baths before long." Sophie sighed.

Addison laughed. "Of that, I have no doubt."

Sophie dropped into the chair at her desk and glanced out the sparkling glass panes. The large dormer window let in so much light it made the attic room less foreboding.

"Shouldn't we be bathing them and getting them ready for the party?" Addison asked.

"Nah, they've already started without us. I say we wait until right before. The kids will scream for a minute. We'll get the girls cleaned up and let them loose again to get messy right after the pictures."

"Devious. I like it. Okay, then. I won't stress," Addison said.

"They are fine. Let them be for a while." Sophie laughed.

"Good. To be honest, I haven't had nearly enough downtime to get caught up again."

"Well, then, get back to work. Marte and Agnes have the crumb snatchers covered," Sophie said.

"Thank you. I'm sorry. I know we are supposed to be here to relax and celebrate."

"And we will. There is plenty of time for that. I have some work I should get caught up on, too." Sophie reached for the stack of files on the corner of her desk and began rifling through them.

They sat in comfortable silence for another hour before they cleaned up their desks and headed downstairs to wrangle the children into clean clothes.

As the last picture was snapped and the last toast cheered, Sophie stood off to the side, enjoying the small piece of cake Claude brought to her.

"What do you say about a little vacation, just the two of us?" he asked.

Sophie shook her head. "The last vacation we took ended in disaster. I don't think I have the energy for another round."

Claude wrapped an arm around her waist and

leaned in close. "I think Adryanna needs a brother," he practically purred.

"And how does that have anything to do with a vacation?"

A wide grin split his face. "That's how we got the last one, isn't it?"

Sophie choked on the piece of cake in her throat.

"We can go to the country house," Claude murmured.

"That sounds safe enough."

"Walk in the gardens of Diana?"

"Yes, that would be nice."

"Make love in the pool under the moon like before…"

"Hmm…" she moaned as he kissed her neck just below her ear.

The idea of getting away did sound nice. The last two years had been a whirlwind of drama. It would be good for them to spend some time alone to get back what they once shared before the accident took his memories away. Every day he remembered a little more of their life together.

"Well, we are overdue for a redo honeymoon," she said.

Sophie leaned into Claude's embrace as he continued to whisper in her ear, distracting her from her daughter's attempts to smear cake all through her hair.

Her life was falling back into place. The love of her life was home where he belonged, his memory returning a little more each day. Sophie had all but given up hope she'd ever experience the love and happiness she longed for. She'd anticipated those things as a given after they had exchanged their vows.

"*Oui*, I think an escape to the country is just what the doctor ordered."

As contentment washed through her, Sophie sighed at the jovial scene before her. Tilting her head back, she kissed her husband under his chin.

THANK YOU FOR PICKING UP A COPY OF ***HIS Heart's Promise*** and giving it a read. I would love your feedback so please feel free to leave me a review here: ***Amazon Review***.

Did you like ***Sophie and Claude's Story***.
Then you'll ***LOVE Book 1*** of this series,
Her Guarded Heart.

Addison and Sergei's Story.

She smothered her hopes with guilt. He still bears scars from old wounds. Can their sweet kisses create a healing transformation?

ADDISON TETRICK REFUSES TO BECOME HER mother. Struggling to keep boundaries between herself and her drama queen of a parent, the frustrated college student seizes a chance to head to Russia for a semester abroad. But when her bubbly French roommate drags her to a local club, she didn't expect her first night in a new country to include an instant attraction to a tall and handsome stranger.

Sergei Petrova is besotted. Delighted to realize the beautiful foreigner is enrolled at his university, the distracted scholar impulsively signs up for a classic literature class while he works up the nerve to introduce himself. And though he can tell she's hopelessly out of his league, the brooding physics major vows to move mountains to win her over.

Certain that lowering her defenses will derail her career, Addison fights the pull of his gorgeous smiles. And hopeful that his sincerity will break down any barriers, Sergei ignores the hints that his beloved is being pushed to her limits.

Can this star-crossed pair turn passion and practicality into an unbreakable formula?

Her Guarded Heart is the vivid first book in the Letting Love In Women's Romantic Fiction series. If you like fun matchmaking, multicultural settings, and coming-of-age stories, then you'll adore Dawn Baca's emotional connection.

Read ***Her Guarded Heart*** to storm the walls of forever today!

———

Do you like ***FREEBIE*** books?
Sign up for my newsletter and get
His Heart's Burden *for Free!*

To read my blog, get the latest news, future release dates, or to join my ARC team sign up for my newsletter at *www.DawnBaca.com.*

Also by Dawn Baca

Acknowledgments

Words could never convey the depths of my gratitude. To my amazing critique partners and editors, who are not only fantastic friends but also amazing authors in their own right:

RB Austin, Esti Bega, Jane Balfrey, Jessica Ripley, Rachel Lamb, Bonnie Phelps, Elsa Bayley, Michelle Remy, Amy Trunoske, Lorri Taylor, Jennifer Dargel, and Sherry Breinig.

To the blurb gods Best Page Forward, for the amazing back of the book, and the amazing graphic artists at 100 Covers for the beautiful cover. To Amabel Daniels, and Deelylah Mullin, my amazing editors who worked their magic to make it shine.

Thank you to Sherry Franssen Breinig and Jennifer Sosh who helped fix the errors that you came across. You ladies help me make the world go round.

This book would not be half of what it is today without all of your love, dedication and support. Thank you for helping me keep the faith and for making my writing better and stronger, and for all of the hard work that went into shaping this story into the best it could be.

Love to you all,
Dawn

About the Author

An insatiable reader of all genres since her childhood, Dawn is a globetrotter hungry to discover new places and experience unique adventures.

She can be found indulging in her husband's first love of summer camping in the mountains or luxuriating in the open seas while cruising to exotic destinations during the frigid winter months.

When she's not jet-setting she can be found in Central Valley California with her family and their many rescue animals.

To read my blog, get the latest news, future release dates, or to join my ARC team sign up for my newsletter at *www.DawnBaca.com.*

facebook.com/DawnMBaca

x.com/BacaDawn

youtube.com/DawnBaca

pinterest.com/dawnmbaca

instagram.com/dawnbaca

amazon.com/author/dawnbaca

bookbub.com/profile/dawn-baca

goodreads.com/dawnbaca

tiktok.com/@bacadawn

Paperback ISBN: 978-1-7329615-2-4
Cover: 100 Covers
Blurb: Best Page Forward
Editor: Wendee Mullikin
Chapter Image by Soukeine on Cleanpng

❀ Created with Vellum